Cyber Spooks

CW00828725

Eliza Jane Goés

Illustrations by Gina Rahman

ISBN: 978-0-244-85453-9

www.publishnation.co.uk

For my two lovely grandchildren, a very different Poppy and Ralph, the pupils at Hendon School who read the first few chapters and my fellow writers in the Finchley Greenacre 'Finish that Novel' group and at Swanwick, The Writers' Summer School, who have been so supportive.

Also, for all those young people who perhaps struggle with the effects of too much time on their smartphones. Like other things, a smartphone can be a good servant but a bad master. Stay happy, eat wisely, keep active, go walking, listen to the birds, smell the flowers, and most importantly, sleep well, if you can, in a room away from screens.

Chapters   Page

Chapter 1:
It isn't me

Brent Cross Shopping Centre, October 30th 2013

As we head homewards towards the escalator to the car park, something hairy tickles my face and my little brother Ralph screams. We've walked into a silvery web with a fat spider and there are more all around. High above us the ceiling is festooned with black cats, witches on brooms and gigantic orange pumpkins. The shops are full of raspberry-liquorice skulls, pus-filled zombie bubble gum, severed fingers, ghostbuster popping candy, jelly eyeballs and mini-chocolate nearly everything Halloweenish. Mum has bought a giant hamper with them all, as it's my birthday tomorrow.

Then I see her!

There isn't a mirror but I'm staring into *my* face, mouth open, eyes boring into mine. I know it's my face, but it isn't me. And that's not my school uniform she's wearing.

This other 'me' doesn't speak and nor do I. A cold draught cuts through my bones and I open my mouth to say something. But what? 'Hello Me?' How stupid is that? We stand rooted to the spot somewhere between fear and disbelief, dream and reality. Can anyone else smell burning?

It takes a few seconds to dawn on me that we're passing each other on up-and-down escalators, which have stuck. Now that's weird. We're right opposite each other, suspended in limbo. There's a shudder, someone screams, and we start moving again, me up, she down. We watch each other float away, swallowed up by shoppers. I miss the end of the moving steps and stumble into my mum's back as I try to get a last glimpse of her.

'What's wrong, Poppy? You look like you've seen a ghost.'

'I think I have, Mum – my own ghost.'

'You can't have a ghost, stupid. You're not actually dead yet,' says my little brother Ralph. He's got a point. 'Actually' is his favourite word right now.

'Didn't you see her on the escalator when it stopped?'

'See who?'

'That girl – she looks just like me.'

'You're trembling,' Mum says. 'Hey. It was just some stranger who looks like you, I'm sure. They say we all have a double somewhere.'

'No, it was me. I looked into her eyes. She knew she was me, too.'

'An actual loony sister. That's all I need.'

'Ralph, be quiet,' Mum says. 'Look, it's been a long day. We shouldn't have come shopping straight from school. Poppy, you're tired. Your mind's playing tricks.'

'No. I saw myself.'

'You're scaring me, Poppy,' Ralph says. 'Let's go home, I'm hungry.' It's unusual for Ralph to be the hungry one. That's usually me.

I can't help thinking Mum has a strange look on her face as she bundles the shopping and us into the car and we roar off. I'm excited. We've got loads of party food, pizzas (and, of course, some healthy stuff to please Mum), a giant birthday cake and little apples for bobbing. We've already got a pumpkin lantern and twenty-four orange and black witchy cupcakes at home. I can't believe I'm thirteen tomorrow. And Dad's fixed up ultraviolet lights and we're all going to wear something white and a Halloween mask. And there's an orange and black piñata full of fang-tastic gummies and wearing a green witch's hat. Ralph thinks that's cool and he can't wait to bash it.

But why can I still see *her* face? I shut my eyes because I don't want Ralph to say I'm crazy again. All I can see is that face, but it's hazy now. I struggle to remember what I saw. Was it a long, baggy, brown dress with shoe laces on the sleeves? There was something about her hair; it was straggly and bumpy, not untidy but not straight and shiny with ginger bits like mine. Was she wearing a brown bow in her brown hair, which didn't show? No, it wasn't me. Yet, her eyes were mine; not many people have hazel eyes with green flecks. I wish I'd looked for the butterfly birthmark like mine on her cheek. And I can't forget that smoky, choking smell.

I'm freezing again. It's like something is stealing my warmth. We get home and I tell Mum I need to lie down. I'm not sleepy but I've so got to sort my brain out.

'All right, dear. You'd better get some rest before your big birthday.'

'Oh yeah, cool. I'd almost forgotten.' I feel a bit better for a moment.

It's Friday so I stuff my school uniform in the laundry basket before Mum nags again that I've left it on the floor. I slip on leggings and the cleanest T- shirt I can find and fling myself on my bed, earphones in with the sound full up. But she's still there. I can hear her voice now, wailing through 'What Makes You Beautiful'. Even my favourite One Direction can't drown the voice out. *'Po...ppy, I know you can hear me. POPPY, speak to me!'*

I rip out the earphones and sit up.

'What do you want?' I croak, not expecting an answer.

'We've been waiting for such a long time.'

'What do you mean? How long?'

'It had to be exactly the first October 31st of a century, like my birth date.'

'But that's *my* birthday, too.'

'I know.'

'How?'

'I know everything about you, so we chose that date.'

'Why? And how can you *choose* it?'

'You'll have to do some waiting now. It's not quite time.'

'Time for what?'

'Wait and see!'

'Float off disembodied voice! You're *so* not real.' OMG, Uncle Tom was taken to hospital when he kept hearing voices.

'Wrong, Daddy's Pops. I *so* am real. Later.'

The bedroom window rattles and I stick my earphones back in. I reckon she won't come back and if she does, she'll go away if I don't speak to her. How does she know Dad calls me Pops?

Perhaps Mum's right and I'm tired. What if I've got the hearing voices thing? They gave Uncle Tom the chemical cudgel, Dad says. I wonder if that hurt. Every time we saw him after that he seemed just dozy – but happy, I suppose.

'Dad's home and supper's ready,' Ralph yells in my ear, 'so you can stop chatting to your mates on the phone, Mum says. Yak, yak, yak – that's all you girls do. Come on, I'm starving.'

'I wasn't chat...' I begin. Oops. Perhaps I'd better keep quiet.

Supper is chicken and wholemeal pasta bake so I feel warm and safe again. Even so, I find myself asking, 'Dad, how old was Uncle Tom when he started hearing voices?'

Mum's got that funny look on her face again – and did she and Dad exchange glances?

Chapter 2:
Next Morning

I wake up to the sound of the doorbell and rush downstairs, thinking it must be the postman with mountains of parcels. It's not every day you become a teenager.

'It's my birthday,' I tell him as he hands me one disappointingly small parcel and a pile of envelopes.

'So I can see.'

'I'm thirteen today.'

'Happy Birthday, old lady.'

'Thanks. Pff.' I give him a look that says 'whatever'.

I decide to keep Voice out of the day. She didn't come back last night but I suppose she didn't get much chance as I was on the phone all the time. Seven boys and seven girls are invited to my party but Wayne's got that norovirus. Yuk. That makes thirteen, unlucky for some. Maybe Ralph can invite Charlie instead of him going to Charlie's house. Perhaps not – they're only six.

'Dad, Mum, can I open my presents now?'

Dad comes out from behind his newspaper and gives me a birthday smacker on the cheek. 'Happy Birthday, Teenybopper.'

'Ugh, don't call me that!'

'Happy Birthday, Poppy,' Mum says and gives me a big hug. 'I reckon it's a great idea to open your presents so we can put them away before you get more tonight.' She might not be my real mum but she's a good one, though she's far too tidy for me. I often wonder what my real mum would have been like – if she hadn't died when I was born. All I know is she had red hair and green eyes. Dad says I'm a mixture of that and his dark hair and dark eyes.

Mum hauls a big bag of parcels out of its hiding place under the stairs just as Ralph crashes in with a crumpled half-wrapped parcel. 'Wait for me! Here you are, Big Sis. Open mine first.'

'It looks nearly open to me.'

'No, it's just not quite closed. I hope you like it.'

'Oh wow, Top Model T-shirt designer and Top Model tattoos. Well done, little brother. I love them.'

'Just don't kiss me, right.'

'No chance.'

'Anyway, they were the first thing on Amazon for thirteen-year-old girls.'

'You can bring Charlie to my party, if you like.'

'No way. Charlie and I have plans.'

'Fine.'

I don't know why, but I'm feeling there are too many unlucky thirteens around. I suppose Voice would make it fourteen.

'Come on, then. Let's open the rest of the presents,' Mum says, probably dying to tidy everything away.

I love my loot! I got a beanie hat with Poppy on it, panda slipper boots, two chocolate twister games, new pyjamas for the sleepover tonight, (a pity the boys aren't allowed to stay), lip gloss in six flavours – mango's the best – and loads of other stuff. I like my cool handbag and the cinema vouchers, but I'm not so sure about Granny's pink cardigan which she knitted herself. Grandma and Grandpa Australia have sent a boomerang and a cuddly Koala backpack, which is what you might expect.

My bestie, Katie, drops by with a funny card and some skinny jeans which *will* fit because we're the same size; we're both a bit tall but she's blonde and blue eyed.

7

'Thanks everyone. What a great birthday so far. Is there any toast left?'

For some reason, I don't tell Katie about Voice. I'd hate it if she didn't understand.

After she goes home, the day goes by in a flurry as we get food, games, music and everything else ready for the evening. I decide I'm going to be a white witch in an old sheet and a fluorescent green hat so I shine in the blue light. It's my party, after all!

I'm hoping one more guest pulls out so we're twelve and not thirteen. When did I get so superstitious?

They'll soon be here and all's well.

'Where's Pippa?' Voice pipes up from nowhere. *'She should be here.'*

I decide to pretend I haven't heard her but I find myself asking Mum and Dad who Pippa is. I watch the colour drain from Mum's face and Dad push his hand through his thick dark hair which he does when he's uncomfortable.

'I thought you'd forgotten all that nonsense,' Dad says. 'Don't you remember? She was your imaginary friend when you were little.'

'Oh, yes, I do sort of remember.' I feel relieved; Voice is just my imaginary childhood friend. She went away before and she will again.

Chapter 3:
The Halloween Birthday Party

All the girls and some of the boys arrive wearing a Halloween mask and something white to glow in the ultraviolet light.

Katie's got white leggings, a black T-shirt with a big white spider's web, and a spider monster mask. Pretty scary, even with her fair hair and her kissy mouth.

Corinne's got white trainers and white gloves; everything else is black except for a white scream mask below her teased-out Afro and she's making everybody laugh by doing a silly dance.

Charlotte's got a white hat and crop top that she looks great in, and Sarah's got a lacy top with a white bra showing. Well, I suppose she's got big enough boobs to show off. Some of us still have to wait, like little Mary dressed as a pumpkin.

Anyway, I'm glad I'm the only one all in white because it's my party and I'll shine if I want to.

Some of the boys are looking bored with this ultraviolet thing but Sean's loving it. He's dressed like an Italian waiter in a white shirt open to the waist and a gold medallion. He even has a disgusting false hairy chest. Gross! His mask is Jedward, not exactly Halloween but I suppose he reckons he's sexy. 'Am I John or am I Edward?' he asks and we all say, 'Who cares? Same as, same as.'

Jonathan, who's still got a bit to grow, looks great in a skeleton costume and mask with all his bones shining white. We tell him he looks great but he's still too shy to join in much.

'When are we going to play spin the bottle?' Sean yells. He can't wait to snog a girl, any girl. I suppose we'd better play. We do and nearly every girl gets snogged, well, pecked quickly, somewhere near the face, but I get Sean and he tries to chew my mouth off. I'm not sure if I'm ready for romance.

Mum's done well for my big birthday. As well as pizza slices, as a surprise she's made hot-dog mummies with pastry wrapped round sausages and yellow eyes from mustard and we add tomato-ketchup blood for ourselves. We're drinking cherryade for Frankenstein's blood with jellied eyeballs and maggots, and after this we'll be ducking for apples and then scoffing the witchy and pumpkin cupcakes and my birthday cake. What a day!

Time's moving on and we're all beginning to dry out from ducking for apples in the kitchen. Mary's curled up on the sofa in her pumpkin suit, fast asleep. I put on my favourite One Direction album *Up All Night* and we dance.

'Look at them,' Dad says to Mum, loud enough for us all to hear, as they check in on us. 'They sway about a bit and call it dancing. Okay guys, only the girls get to stay and there's going to be no up all night for them, either.'

'Aw, Mr Danford, just a bit longer,' Corinne says politely, knowing I'd probably not get away with persuading my own dad.

'Right, half an hour, no longer. Start ringing home for lifts, boys.'

It's been great and the girls are looking forward to getting into their pyjamas later on. We can have a good gossip. I turn the lights low and leave the blue light on and carry on dancing.

'Wow! How did you do that? Spooky!!!' Sean says.

Everyone gasps. Mary wakes up and screams.

'Do what?' I say.

'There's two of you! The other you is floating above you!'

And she is, and dressed exactly like me, but there's no sign of Voice. I panic. I pretend I'm pretending to be spooked and laugh loudly. I can't tell everybody I keep seeing and hearing things.

As quickly as she came, she's gone. Thank goodness. I feel myself taking a deep breath.

'Go on. Tell us how you did that.'

'Sorry, I can't tell you.'

'Please!'

'No, it's a Magic Circle secret.'

'Cool.'

'Wicked.'

'Awesome.'

Jonathan's dad arrives to take him home and drop off four of the other boys, and Sean sets off walking because he lives around the corner.

We girls giggle as we get into our pyjamas. I'm hoping Voice doesn't come or, if she does, that I'm the only one who can hear her.

Katie starts. 'Shall we play "Would I lie to you?" or "Would you rather?"'

My friends' voices seem far away and I can't get excited over the boy gossip. It turns out Corinne has the hots for Sean and she's dead jealous I was the one who got kissed.

'You can have him, Corinne. I'm not bothered,' I tell her.

11

'Really? I thought you liked him.'

'Naw.'

It seems we're playing 'Would you rather?'

Katie continues, 'Would you rather sleep on the floor or four in a bed … erm … Mary?'

'Can't I have Ralph's bed in the next room?' says Mary, 'I'm cream crackered.'

'No, it's one room for all or it spoils the fun,' I tell them.

'I'll sleep here, then,' says Mary, making that four on my bed, two on the sofa bed and one on the airbed.

'Oh my God, I think she's asleep already,' Katie says. 'Right, try again. Poppy, would you rather … erm … eat worms or … erm … kiss Sean?

'Easy. Eat worms. Corinne, same question.'

'That's not fair. You know the answer.'

'Okay. Would you rather kiss Sean or go on a month's holiday in the sun?'

'Oh, that's easy. I'll have the holiday.'

'See! It's not true love, then.'

'Girls,' my mother calls out. 'Don't get too tired. It'll spoil tomorrow.' How did she get to be such an an*noy*ing mum? I bet everything in the kitchen is embarrassingly clean by now too.

'Okay, Mrs Danford,' someone shouts and we dissolve into whispered guffaws.

'Would you rather,' Charlotte whispers, 'be a boy or a girl? Everybody.'

'Definitely a girl because we get to have a sleepover.'

'A girl – not so daft as a boy,' pipes up Corinne.

'A boy – they get to go out more – well, my brother does…' Charlotte adds.

It's morning and the sprawled bodies are beginning to stir.

'You snore, Mary. My God, I couldn't get to sleep!'

'I don't snore.'

12

'How do you know? You're asleep when you do.'

'Joke too old,' Mary replies.

'And Poppy, you talk in your sleep.' Katie says.

'Yeah, I heard you too but it's like you have two voices,' says Corinne.

'What?' I say. This is a bit scarier than they know.

'I heard you calling "Penelope, Penelope," in a funny voice and then you yelled, "My name's NOT Penelope," and you sounded really peed off.'

'Maybe you were dreaming about that ghost you made with the lights or whatever last night,' Charlotte adds.

'Maybe,' I say and I can feel myself shaking. Nobody asks me again about the ghostly double because Mum calls and breaks the spell. Saved.

'Pancakes ready in ten minutes, girls. Mary, your mother's here; we're having coffee but she says she can't wait forever.'

Chapter 4:
Tell me What?

I'm thirteen and two days now. Fancy that. It was a great birthday, apart from Voice and Spook and the dream I didn't remember. Sometimes you can remember dreams if you wake up and tell someone straightaway or even write them down. Mostly I forget, but perhaps I need to concentrate on remembering now that Voice might be speaking to me. I'm scared but, you know, I'm more than a bit excited too, like I'm at the beginning of a new adventure.

I need some breakfast.

'Do you think we should tell her?' Mum is saying.

'I'm not sure. I'm wondering if she's ready. Look what happened to her mother's brother.'

I don't mean to eavesdrop but I'm upset that there's some secret I might not be ready to learn about. 'Tell me what?' I ask coming downstairs and into the kitchen. 'You shouldn't speak so loudly.'

'Oh, uh. It's just a treat we're planning for you and Ralph for the … erm … summer holidays.'

'You can't fool me, Mum. It's got something to do with Uncle Tom. I heard that. Dad, you'll tell me the truth.'

'All right, I will. Get your breakfast first and come and sit down. '

We sit down after I get my cereal. I'm quiet for once.

Dad finally begins. 'You know that your mother, Stella … well, she died when you were born. You know that. What we didn't tell you was that you have … had … a twin. She … she's…'

'She's no longer with us,' Mum Rosie adds quickly. 'The reason we're telling you now is we think your twin has been trying to contact you – or her spirit has, I mean.'

'I know that sounds crazy,' Dad adds, 'but when you were little you used to play and talk endlessly to this imaginary friend. The strange thing was that you called her Pippa, and that was the name that Stella called your twin. Stella kept saying things like, "My twins will grow up happy," and, "My spirit will keep them together." This was after she thought she was dying. It was so heartbreaking. I didn't know what I was doing. Your Uncle Tom was there to support me and we took turns sitting with her. The doctors thought she'd make it but she haemorrhaged. She'd been crying out for some herb or other which was the only thing that could save her. The young doctor said he'd never use that as it was poison, and that she was hallucinating, and they didn't manage to save her.

'Oh, Dad, that must have been just horrible for you.' I'm not telling him I'm feeling sick and shaky myself. He looks even more upset than I am.

'You and Pippa were so dependent on me then...'

'Pippa was ... taken away,' Mum says.

'Thank you, Rosie... I couldn't bring myself to say that,' Dad croaks.

'Why didn't you tell me she'd died?' I can't help asking. My question is ignored.

'Then you, Poppy,' Dad carries on, 'were my reason to live. I was happy that you had an imaginary friend, and she stayed with you until you were five and then she seemed to go away when you went to school and met new friends. After five years, Rosie and I decided to marry and then Ralph came along. We thought that was the end of Pippa.'

'But I thought it was my own ghost, not my twin's. Oh, I'm so confused.'

15

'You saw her on the escalator at Brent Cross, didn't you?' Ralph says, beside himself with excitement. He's been doing a bit of eavesdropping on the stairs too, I guess.

'Oh Ralphy, I'm sorry. Did you hear all that?' says Mum, reaching out to put an arm around his shoulder. 'You mustn't be scared.'

I see Mum, Dad and Ralph, their three dark heads huddled together and I feel different, the odd one out. A freak who sees ghosts and hears voices.

'I'm not scared! It's cool that my sister has a real ghost,' Ralph says. 'Poppy, I'm sorry I didn't believe you. Wait till I tell Cha—'

'Now hang on, Ralph,' Dad says. 'Don't you dare go telling Charlie or anybody else about this! People might not understand. Do you hear?'

Ralph's face is crumpling. 'Aw, Dad... Oh, all right then. I suppose they might think...'

I'd better tell them everything, about Voice, the second white witch floating on the ceiling and the dream where Voice, now my dead twin Pippa, I suppose, was calling me Penelope. Mum and Dad don't seem surprised but Ralph's mouth looks like it is about to catch flies. I ask Dad if I was ever called Penelope.

'No, Stella insisted on Poppy and Pippa. She didn't want the name Philippa either. I remember thinking how strange it was that she felt so strongly. Poppy, I'm sorry I...'

'Don't be sorry. You've been the bestest dad, ever. If she comes again, I'm going to ask her if her name is Philippa or Pippa.'

'I bet she never comes back now that we know all about her,' Ralph says. 'We can wave silver crosses and garlic around and tell her to float off!'

'She's not a vampire, idiot!'

16

I give Dad and Mum a big, warm hug. Dad's trying not to cry and Mum is looking very bleak. I hope Ralph is right, that Pippa's never coming back, but there's still something drawing me towards my dead twin and pulling me into the unknown. Is this what paranormal means? I must Google it.

Chapter 5:
Uncle Tom

January 2014

We're into another year and Voice, sorry, Pippa, hasn't been around since my birthday so it's good she didn't spoil Christmas. Result! Ralph has put a silver cross on my bedroom door which he's sure is doing the trick and keeping her away. I told him to read Mary Shelley's *Frankenstein* but he says it's too long. Well, I suppose he's only seven.

'That's what you normally do to scare off ghosts, isn't it?' he says.

The only one outside the family I've told about Pippa is my best friend, Katie. I wanted to miss out the bit about my twin who died as that's too real and scary, but I told her. She got the heebie-jeebies at first but we've been Googling like mad about separated twins and the paranormal and ghosts and things; we found this word *reincarnation* which means born again and I am *so* not sure that Pippa doesn't want to steal my body to put her spirit in it so she can live my life. Then what would I do? If she comes into my body, my body will be the same and nobody will know; but then I'll be a spirit wandering around looking for another body. Katie says she'll probably like Pippa just as well as she likes me, and she'll definitely know if it's not me because she won't know our special secrets.

'I think she knows all our secrets; she knows *everything*,' I say.

'So you really think she'll come back, don't you, Poppy?'

'I'm not sure. If she steals me, I'll come and be your imaginary friend,' I promise.

'That's really scary. Just don't *say* that. Anyway, she hasn't been around for ages. She's probably gone,' Katie sort of squeaks.

The rest of the world have been talking about that spooky Halloween trick so Ralph, Katie, Dad and Rosie Mum (I'd better call her that in case Stella Mum's a spirit too) have cooked up a story about a video we prepared earlier, and a hidden projector we set up to scare everyone. The people at my party seem to believe it, Dad reckons. I hope so; I'd rather be called clever than freaky.

Uncle Tom has just arrived. I can see his taxi outside. He's been in Australia visiting his other sister who went there because of the shock after my mum died. Grandma and Grandpa, Uncle Tom's (and Stella Mum's) parents are there, too. I wish they weren't so far away. I only see them on Skype. Uncle Tom's got a new job in London with a mobile phone company or he says he wouldn't be leaving the January sun.

He seems to have got over the hearing voices thing. I wonder if Stella Mum was the one speaking to him and he couldn't tell anyone. Katie and I looked up 'hearing voices' and got loads of info on good voices and bad voices and the reasons for hearing them or seeing visions. I really don't think poor Uncle Tom should have had the chemical cudgel.

I suppose I'd better go downstairs, though I don't mind Uncle Tom. I've always liked him and I think he likes me. We have a *definity,* see, or is that affinity? Anyway, we seem to understand each other.

I've never seen Uncle Tom look better; he's very tanned and his auburn hair has lighter bits that might have been bleached in the sun. All this seems to be making his green eyes even greener. Dad is asking how Grandma, Grandpa, Sal, John and the kids are and Uncle Tom's telling us they are all well. Little Susie is five now and Robbie is nearly three, and they spend all their free time on the beach.

'Hi, Uncle Tom,' I say. 'How was Australia for you?'

'Sunny and lots of loud people, but I've never felt better.' I look into his face and I think perhaps he means the voices haven't been getting to him.

'Sometimes it's good to be really far away - from everything, I mean,' I say, just to check.

'I know what you mean, Poppy. What about you? How does it feel to be a teenager? Thirteen's a really big deal, eh?' His big eyes seem to be looking right through me.

Ralph butts in where he isn't wanted, as usual. 'Hey, did you hear about the spooky Halloween party where Poppy's twin came floating in? My birthday last week was really boring. It's not fair.'

'Did she now?' Uncle Tom says, staring into space. He is *not* being the patronising uncle indulging seven-year-old Ralph. In fact, he doesn't seem one bit surprised. He looks at Dad and asks, 'Does she know?'

'About Pippa? Yes. She was sorry to hear Pippa had … died.'

'Oh … I see. Right then, we'll leave it at that.'

'Uncle Tom, it's okay,' I say. 'I think her spirit must have been my imaginary friend until I was five. She came for a day or two round my birthday but she's gone again. I'm not scared … I think.'

'Even if she does come back she means you no harm, so don't you worry.'

'Tea,' Rosie Mum calls, bringing in a tray of mugs and a plate of biscuits.

'Hobnobs,' Ralph shouts and the spell is broken. I'll talk to Uncle Tom alone later.

'I have some good news,' Uncle Tom says. 'A lovely lady has agreed to be my wife. Can you believe that? She's been a friend of your Auntie Sal for years and we came back on the same flight. Simon, you might remember Celia.'

20

'Oh yes, blue black hair and light blue eyes. Congratulations,' Dad says and shakes his hand.

'Thanks, Simon. I'll bring her to visit soon. You'll like her, I know. She's a psychiatrist.' We all hug cuddly Uncle Tom, happy that he's happy about his new fiancée.

I catch Uncle Tom drying the tea mugs when nobody else is around.

'How do you know Pippa's coming back?' I ask

'Stella, or her spirit, speaks to me but I don't tell just anyone. I don't want people putting labels on me.'

'Like schizophrenic or psychotic or stuff?'

'Please don't breathe a word. Promise?' Uncle Tom says with a look between surprise and fear on his face.

'Okay, I promise.'

'Celia knows. She understands and she's not going to tell a soul.'

'Good. I feel so much better now that the family knows, and my friend Katie. Only Ralph is a bit of a dangerous blabbermouth. What does Stella – or is it her ghost – say?'

'She wants her twins to grow up together and she loves you both very much. She's asked me to keep an eye on you – that kind of thing. So, Poppy, if you ever have a problem, remember you can always come and talk to me.'

'Thanks. I really need someone who understands.'

'If I were you, I'd let everybody think Pippa has gone forever. Don't tell them if she contacts you again. Okay?'

'Okay, Uncle Tom, but can I tell you?'

'Of course, that's what I'm here for as your guardian spirit linking you with your mother.'

'How long does it take two people to wash up five mugs? What's up?' Mum Rosie asks as she comes into the kitchen.

'Just chatting, Mum.' Uncle Tom and I both put our fingers on our lips behind her back and rejoin the normal world.

21

Chapter 6:
The Time is Getting Closer

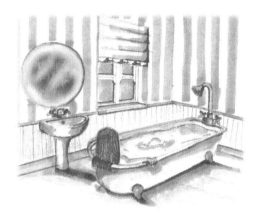

I don't know whether to feel relieved or disappointed. I keep waiting for Pippa but there's no sign of her. Perhaps Uncle Tom really is crazy and she isn't coming back. Katie and I have pretty much stopped Googling and talking about the spooky stuff, but I don't know why I'm still so restless.

Katie's on a homework visit so we can finish our Geography project on tropical rainforests. I'm doing the maps and she's doing the graphs. I suppose we could do another PowerPoint presentation, though Mr Hargreaves is sure to groan and say, 'Not again.'

'Poppy, that wasn't there a minute ago,' Katy says, pointing to a magazine on my bed, which has a thick red ring round a picture of a castle.

'My fairy-tale castle! It's exactly the one I see in my dreams. Dad must have put it there.'

'I don't think so. He's been watching the football since he got home.'

'Look, there's an ad for holiday cottages near an adventure park next to Loch Ness. We should go there and see the monster – and the castle. Let's go and ask Dad if this is our summer holiday.' We go down and interrupt his precious football.

'Dad, this looks fab. Is it our summer holiday?'

'Let me have a look. Where did you find it?'

'I thought you put it on my bed.'

'No, it wasn't me. Rosie, was it you?'

'No, I've never seen it.'

'Ralph?'

'What are you talking about? No.'

Katie and I look at each other. I wonder if she's thinking what I'm thinking.

'Let me have a look,' says Mum Rosie. 'Do you know, Simon, it would be a lovely idea to get this cottage, and it's a very reasonable price. And the cottages are in the grounds of Ballindourie Castle. Have you heard of it?'

'I think I might have. Is it one of those supposedly haunted castles with guided tours?'

'Yes, they mention that.'

'It would have to be the end of July and the beginning of August, but we could think about it. Let me check my dates at work tomorrow. I'll take this ad with me.'

'Can Katie come?' I ask.

'We'd have to ask your parents, Katie, but I can't see why not.' Rosie Mum says.

'What about Charlie?' Ralph asks.

'Not sure yet. Let's see.' Rosie Mum adds, 'We'd need a bigger car. Anyway, don't get your hopes up yet.'

We get back to our homework and nearly finish before we run out of brain power. Katie's mum comes to collect her and

I'm too tired to stay up. I'll be asleep as soon as my head hits the pillow – but I must just have a last look at the castle on the internet. It looks amazing and I *really* hope we can go there.

As I'm drifting off, I think I hear a soft voice. **'The time is getting closer,'** it says, or am I dreaming? I'm too sleepy to respond.

It's 8:30 am and Dad is complaining loudly. Somebody has forgotten to put the extractor fan on and his shaving mirror is steamed up. Rosie's yelling that she *did* put it on. This is the third time this has happened this week, Dad says. Whatever.

I'm staying under the duvet for a bit longer. I've just remembered it's a staff training day. No school. Yippee! And no Ralph because he *has* got school. Even better.

Everyone leaves with Rosie Mum shouting she'll be back in twenty minutes after walking Ralph to school. She's taken time off from the health shop she and Stella Mum started before I was born. I keep telling her I can look after myself now that I'm thirteen, but she's having none of it.

I was wiped out exhausted last night and I still am; my sleep was disturbed as I kept waking up feeling cold and trying to remember my dreams. Fairy castles with herb gardens and a Scottish loch were all mixed up with Pippa on the escalator and Pippa as a floating white witch. I'm going to laze in a long, hot, bubble bath and soak my weariness away.

There *is* something wrong with the extractor fan; you switch it on and it switches itself back off. Oh my God, could it be…? Has Voice turned into a naughty poltergeist?

I'm staring at the mirror as I soak deliciously in the bubbles.

Pippa is missing Poppy appears from nowhere, like an invisible hand is writing on the steamy mirror. I scream but then, after a second, I'm not afraid. It's as if I've been waiting for this moment when my imaginary friend, my twin's spirit, makes contact. I feel no menace and I now believe that Uncle Tom was right when he said Pippa means me no harm.

24

I sink back into the warm bath to watch and listen. No more writing appears but a strange voice, deeper and softer than Pippa's, begins to speak.

'Not long now, Poppy, we've been waiting for far too long."

'Who are you? You're not Pippa. And what have you been waiting for?

'You'll see. It's going to be wonderful, another chance for true happiness.'

'When?'

'Soon, my Poppy.'

I wait and wait but there is nothing more. The bathwater cools and the message in the steam fades away. Funnily enough, the extractor fan has switched itself on again. If it's not Pippa, who *is* this ghost?

Rosie Mum's back, but I'm not going to scare her with this new development. I'll speak to Uncle Tom later.

'I'm back, Poppy.'

'Hi, Mum. I've been thinking. Why don't I come with you to the shop one day? I quite fancy learning about health foods and herbs and stuff.'

'Well, that would be great. I could teach you so much. You could come during half term, if you like, but today Jenny's getting paid to be there and I really need to tackle that mountain of ironing and get this place tidy.'

I think, what's new? Mum doing ironing and tidying that doesn't need to be done.

Ah well, I'll have time to read my Christmas present, *Poppy's Angel* the sequel to *Poppy's Hero*, which I was given *two* copies of as birthday presents. If your name's Poppy, you inevitably get clothes with poppies and two copies of popular books with Poppy in the title. I've discovered Poppy's father is still in prison; it's a good story though I fell asleep reading it

25

last night. It must be exhaustion from all this ghost-infested insomnia.

I can't describe how excited I feel. I'm wondering what's quite so special about a fairytale castle on a loch. Dad gets back from work and says we can book the Loch Ness cottage for two weeks around the end of July into August. I've just rung Katie but she can't come because her cousin's getting married in Canada. Mum says she couldn't possibly handle Charlie and Ralph together for two weeks, especially on the long journeys so it looks like Ralph and I are stuck with each other for company. I don't really mind that Katie can't come or even that I'll have to put up with Ralph 24/7. What I would mind, desperately, would be if we didn't get a booking.

'Dad, go online and book for the four of us ... now... in case all the cottages near the castle go... please.'

'Okay, okay, I will. You're keen aren't you?'

'Yes, well look at that picture. Isn't that castle magical?

'I bet it's haunted,' Ralph adds. I want to say I hope it is but something stops me and the moment disappears as Dad finds the website and books our two weeks from July 26th to August 9th. I hope school's finished by then.

'Happy Pops?'

'Very happy thanks Dad.'

I'm off to my room to dream about ghosts in Ballindourie Castle. I'm beginning to be able to dream at will. Sometimes I'm not sure what's real or what isn't any more. Am I making myself dream or is it something else ... or someone? When my dreams come, I see a woman in a long grey dress with red hair flying behind her as she runs along the bank of a rushing river. She seems desperate. I don't know why.

I haven't managed to chat to Uncle Tom about the new voice but I must.

Chapter 7:
My name is NOT Penelope

It's February half term, Ralph is at Charlie's and I'm helping Mum out at the Health shop like she promised.

I think Mum finds it a bit sad to take me there because she and my real mum used to run it together. She tells me Stella knew all about herbal medicines and was the one who taught her all she knows.

'Did she study healing plants?' I ask.

'She did for a while but she complained that she knew more than her teachers. Your mum was the one who planted all these herbs behind the hedge at the bottom of the garden. I'm afraid a lot of the plants have died off and I don't know their names or where she found them.'

Mum's looking sad so I don't think I'll ask any more questions for the moment but I must go and have a look at that herb garden – I thought it was just a load of weeds down there. Dad never likes us going there and I'm beginning to understand why.

An old woman with a bad shoulder comes into the shop looking for something to rub on it.

'Arnica's good for that,' I say picking a bottle off a shelf.

'*It's from sunflowers and it's poisonous if you eat it, so be careful,*' I find myself saying. Where did that come from? I don't even know if that's true.

'That's right isn't it, Mum,' I add, in case I've got it wrong.

'Have you been learning about natural remedies my dear,' the woman asks, 'so you can help your mother?'

'Erm…,'

'Yes, she has. I'm very proud of her,' Mum adds quickly but when the old lady leaves she's puzzled too.

'Poppy, have you really been looking up herbs?'

'No, and I've no idea *how* I know about arnica. I just do, like I know yarrow is for boils, burdock leaves for grazes and goose fat for burns.

Rosie's jaw is hitting her chin. 'You must have been reading about them.'

'No. Maybe someone told me but I can't remember who or when.'

'What else can you tell me?'

'Mmm – *dried nettles for scurvy and rosehips for bleeding gums and clove oil for toothache – oh and ergot for when a baby is born to stop the mother bleeding.*'

'Whaaaat! I've never even heard of ergot.'

I'm feeling dizzy and I think I'm going to faint. Why is it so cold?

'It's very dangerous if it's used in the wrong way; it can cause St Anthony's fire. Horrible, and I hate, hate, hate it.' I didn't say that.

'Mum, I didn't say that.'

'Say what?'

'Didn't you hear a voice say that ergot is dangerous?'

'I didn't hear that.'

'I must have been dreaming. Don't worry about it.'

'What's the matter Poppy? You're shaking and you're freezing. Are you ill?'

'I think I must be.'

'You're not ill, Penelope. You do know all this and much, much, more. One day you'll find out and it won't be long now.'

'My name is NOT Penelope,' I shout. Why aren't I totally terrified? I'm more excited than scared. I feel sure the voices aren't dangerous; they're friendly and sort of comforting – most of the time.

'Poppy, I never said your name was Penelope. Please, calm down. It's all right.' Mum makes me eat some healthy flapjack with some ginger tea while she carries on serving in the shop. People come in wanting vitamin pills, organic foods, gluten free, dairy free, high fibre foods and slimming tablets. It all seems very strange but, just lately, in some ways very familiar. I feel oddly drawn towards all these potions, pills and foods to make people better. Will this be what I do when I grow up?

When it's time to go home, I'm feeling like Spookland has almost faded away. Mum's voice is chatting about picking up Ralph first before shopping for dinner or shopping first and then picking him up. I tell her I'm not bothered so we shop first in case he's not ready to come quickly. I'm so bored.

When we get home, it's dark and scary so I don't dare go down to the herb patch at the bottom of the garden. It'll be light in the morning.

Chapter 8:
Ringlets in my Hair

Mum's talking to Dad and I'm eavesdropping again. I can't help it if it's so easy to hide half way upstairs. Mum hates closed doors so I can always hear everything.

'Do you know something, Simon?'

'Mm?'

'Poppy seems to have inherited her mother's interest in herbal medicines and the odd thing is that she seems to know some facts she says she didn't find on the internet.'

'I bet she did Google them; she's probably trying to be mysterious and interesting.'

I want to tell them 'did *not*' but it would be good to keep the earwigging going for a while. You never know what you might learn. After a minute of silence, I go into the kitchen.

'Morning.'

'Morning, Pops. What's the plan?

'Can I come to the shop again, Mum? That was fun. Ralph's off out with Charlie today isn't he?'

'Of course you can; I can always use the help.'

Mum and Dad exchange glances but I'm sure they don't know I've noticed.

'Was that you in the garden in your dressing gown earlier on?' Dad asks.

'Oh. I thought everyone was asleep. I just needed some fresh air.'

'Must be 'soon to be spring' fever,' Dad says.

'Or something,' Mum adds.

I'm not going to tell them that 'the something' was to see what was left of Mum's herbal patch. The truth is, not a lot – it just looks like an untidy tangle of weeds, some of them green but most of them dead as it's still winter, but there's something comforting and familiar about the place. There's an exciting smell that I know but can't quite place. You know what it's like when you know a piece of music but not what it's called. Down in that garden behind the high, straggly hedge, smells and sounds were coming at me from somewhere far away and a very long time ago. My mind was floating away.

And I won't tell them about the dreams last night: hazy dreams of a shiny lake with the different sounds of tiny waves lapping on to a grassy bank here or a stony beach there, dreams of sunlight on the water and upside down trees, confusing in my sleepy state until I realised it was the reflection of tall trees growing on the slopes of a steep hill rising up from the far side of this lake, and dreams filled with voices talking nonstop, though the words had disappeared by morning, if I had ever understood them... I feel as if I'm being pulled towards that glistening lake; something tells me I have to go there but I don't know why.

This morning's dream, just before I woke, was different, more like it was really happening; I was walking along a rocky path cut out through long grass mixed with low heather and I was wearing a long, wide, brown skirt which was annoying me because it was stopping me from going faster. There was a heavy white apron over it. My shoes were uncomfortable too – heavy. I touched them and the soles were wooden and the top was hairy like some brown animal. I heard a voice behind me. 'What's wrong?' it said. 'Have you broken your pampooty?' I *think* she said pampooty. Turning round I saw a girl wearing a brown dress with laces tied in bows on her sleeve, a white apron and hairy shoes. I thought it was me for a moment but her hair was a mass of sausage curls tied up on each side of her head. Before I could speak or feel for curls on my head, I woke up! I tried and tried to go back to sleep to finish my dream but it never works, does it?

'You're very quiet this morning, Pops,' Dad says.

'Still sleepy,' I reply.

Ralph comes downstairs looking for breakfast in a hurry as Charlie and his mum are due to pick him up. 'We're going skating at Ally Pally today,' he yells excitedly.

'Wicked,' I manage to groan.

'Mum,' I say as we're driving to the shop. 'Do you think I could do something different with my hair?'

'You mean cut it short?'

'Oh no, I'd hate that. Maybe put it in sausage curls or something.'

'You mean ringlets. I'm not sure I know how. I remember my gran saying she did them, but I don't know how she did it. You're a funny old-fashioned girl, aren't you? '

'No way - lots of celebrities have curls. Haven't you seen Rihanna's curls, or Beyoncé or even oldies you know like Helena Bonham-Carter? They've got curls. Or Emma Roberts?'

'Who's Emma Roberts?'

'Mum! Don't you know she's Julia Roberts' niece?'

'Sorry, No. Why do you suddenly want celebrity curls, anyway? It's not like you.'

'Just thinking,' I say to Mum and the real world - but I've got a picture in my head of this pretty woman in a long green dress and wooden shoes tearing up thin strips of cloth from an old, worn out petticoat. Strips, more strips and more. Long wide strips, all round the hem of the wide skirt, long narrow strips - and now she's tearing them into shorter strips. What is she going to use them for?

'It's nought but an old lockram petticoat,' a voice I think I recognise says. I can hear a baby, just a tiny cry like a newborn, but so, so far away.'

'What did you say, Mum?'

'Nothing.'

I can't seem to wake up this morning; my dreams are still drifting around in my head.

'Anyway, will you help me do ringlets tonight when Katie's over?'

'Sure. We can give it a go.'

The day goes by quickly and I think I'd like to be a herbalist; it must be my thing. This woman who bought the arnica came in saying how great it was, better than anything from Boots. I knew it would be so I told her. Mum gave me that funny look again but I pretended not to notice because the last time I asked her what was wrong, she said I was imagining things. But I wasn't.

I've phoned Katie and asked her if she wants ringlets in her hair and she thinks that's amaze-balls and she'll look it up on YouTube for instructions. I won't tell her it's going to be parent-over-shoulder as I'm sure Mum won't mind being ditched. We're going to have a sleepover so maybe we can leave the curling in all night and go to Brent Cross tomorrow – lookin' cool and doin' some window.

We're on the laptop and we haven't managed to dump Mum who says she wouldn't miss the fun for the world. Katie's chilled about it but I'm bordering on the moody.

'This one's American but you could use old stockings or socks,' Katie suggests as she clicks on a YouTube demo.

'Or these strips of cloth I ripped up,' I say. 'I found a worn out old sheet in the airing cupboard. Oops I hope that's okay.'

'That's fine. I was going to use it for floor cloths anyway. But, when did you do that?' Mum asked, looking puzzled.

'When you were cooking, before Katie arrived and we'll need to wet our hair a bit but not too much.' '*And,*' said the woman on the video, '*you'll need to wet your hair but not too much.*'

How weird is that when you say something and someone repeats it on TV or the radio or YouTube? We decide it's spooky and move on. This American voice carries on with the instructions. We can do that. You just roll up the hair and tie a knot in the rag and leave it to dry. Simple.

'No, no, no – it's seven; five round the top and two at the bottom. And it's up and down, not across. It won't look right. Make two knots to keep them in all night.'

Was that my voice or is the supernatural kicking in again? There's no reaction from Katie or Mum so I must be hearing voices again. I'm not paranoid, am I? No, I'm not scared at all but I don't want them to know what I heard.

'Can we do yours first, Katie? I've seen a better way – somewhere or other, I can't remember where.'

'Absolutely Poppy; I thought you'd be sure to want to be first.'

'Whatever.' I say, wondering if I'm really so selfish, normally.

My fingers are flying through Katie's long, shiny, blonde hair as if they're being guided. First, I'm making a middle parting and taking some hair from the top.

'Not so much. Remember you need five locks from the top, two each side and one in the middle.'

I am the only one to hear that so I start again and soon finish the five locks all facing up and down. Voice hasn't spoken again. I start at the bottom.

'Divide the hair in the middle at the bottom.'

I do it again and manage to make the curls almost vertical and tie double knots in the rags.

'There. That should do it. Now, can you do the same for me?'

'How come you did that so quickly, Poppy?' Mum asked. There's a mixture of respect and fear in her expression.'

'Yea Poppy; that was wicked awesome.'

'That good, eh.' I'd better keep my secret. 'Come on then, do mine now.'

Mum and Katie between them, with a bit of nagging from me, get my curls in, five at the top and two at the bottom and vertical. Something tells me we need to tie something round our heads so Mum digs in a drawer and we laugh at how 'old' we look in her flowery, swirly scarves.

'Nutcases,' was all Ralph could say when we came downstairs for hot chocolate and hobnobs before bed.

'Shuh up, little brother,' I say. 'What do you know about anything?'

'I can't wait until morning,' Katie whispers as we go upstairs.

...

We're feeling so pretty here at Brent Cross and I can't count how many times we've been rubber-necked by the boys. We're one blonde and one brunette looking great in curls. It feels good to ignore the admirers. I can't believe the hair turned out so brilliant. Two scrunchies, one on either side, and the ringlets at the back left to hang naturally. We're unique – well only two of us in the whole world have this style. Edgy we are. Trendy

'Let's go for a veggie burger,' Katie says, so we do and bask in some more admiring stares in the queue. MacDonald's is crowded so we decide to sit on a bench in the centre at the bottom of the escalator. We're munching away when I see her. Not two of us, but three of us with our unique hairstyle, except she has red ribbons in hers instead of scrunchies. I can't see what she's wearing below the waist because she's hidden by the side of the escalator.

'Look Katie. She looks exactly like me, with our new hairstyle.' I point frantically but Katie can't see her. 'You must be able to see her.' The escalator has stopped and people are looking surprised.

'I can't see anything, Poppy. Are you ok? Poppy?' I pull out my phone and point and click. Got her.

'See, Katie!' The image is as clear as daylight in my photo gallery.

'It can't be you, Poppy but... Oh My God!' Her face goes as white as a sheet and we hang on to each other, shaking with cold, or is it fear? 'She's got your birthmark! It *is* you.'

'I thought it was only in my mind but now I have the proof.'

Chapter 9:
Cyber Spook

'She's staring straight at us Poppy! Why didn't I see her?'

'I don't know …yet, but I'm gonna WhatsApp this to my dad. He's not sure whether it's all in my mind but now he'll have to believe me. Katie, promise me you won't tell anyone about this. I couldn't bear it.'

There's no way I want to share this load of stuff on Facebook.

'Trust me Poppy, I'm your best friend and your secret's safe with me.'

'Thanks. It's just that it's scaring me out of my socks.'

The image has gone to Dad's smartphone. I wonder what he'll think. Maybe he'll say it was just me dressing up and Katie using my phone.

'Poppy?'

'Yes, Katie?'

'Do you think it's a ghost? And do you think she wants to harm you? It might be evil and try to possess you. You know, like ...'

'Like what? No, I'm not scared of her; she's not an 'it' and I'm sure she wants to be friends. I think she might be the ghost of my twin, Pippa.'

'The twin who died?' Katie's eyes and mouth are wide open.'

'I think she's the voice and she's been writing messages in the bathroom steam and she told me how to do ringlets and I even think my dead mum has been telling me about herbs and things. Dad seems so gutted when we talk about my mum and twin so I didn't tell anyone, not even you. Sorry. I should have told you.'

'Yes you should. Well, I'm glad I know now. But don't keep anything else from me. OK? Promise?'

'Promise.'

I send it to Katie's phone too so we can both have proof. She's downloading it now.

'That's funny Pop, it's all blurry.' And it is. The shape is there but there's a bright light where the face should be, like a giant candle flame.

'There must be something wrong with your phone,' I tell her. I send her an old image of Ralph which downloads perfectly so her phone is good.

'No,' she gasps and we both panic. This is some techie ghost if she did this. I open my gallery again and there she is - a perfect image. How? Why? But we do have the evidence. I've got a double!

38

My phone rings. It's Dad and he wants to know why I've sent a duff picture of myself with that silly hairstyle. I tell him it wasn't duff when I sent it. He wonders why.

'Later Dad,' I say. 'It's complicated.'

'Do you think it'll download on to the laptop?' Katie asks.

'I don't know anything anymore.'

...

Back at home, Mum and Dad are giving each other that funny look again. They've seen the clear image on my phone and there's been a long silence.

'Do you mind if I show this to Uncle Tom, Poppy?' Dad asks.

'No, but why?'

'Well, he might have some sort of explanation because I have to say I am very confused.'

'Do you mean because he's such an expert in computers?'

'Maybe, but more because he claims to be in touch with…well you know…'

'Ghosts you mean, Dad, like my mother and my twin.'

'Well…perhaps…'

Mum adds, 'I think we'd better not tell Ralph, darling. He wouldn't be scared but he might start spreading silly stories.'

'You're right Mum,' I say but I don't add that I think he *would* be scared. Like me he'd see 'she' is real, whoever or whatever 'she' is.

Dad hovers nervously over his smartphone but leaves it on the table and phones Uncle Tom on the landline.

Hi Tom, can you spare some time before dinner? There's something I want to ask you.'

We sit in silence again, glad that Ralph is at Charlie's house, until Uncle Tom's car draws up outside and he breezes in.

'What's up?' he asks.

'WhatsApp, that's what's up,' I say, chuffed with my word play. 'Look at this.'

39

'A picture of you. So?'

'Now look at this on my phone,' says Dad.

'There's something wrong with your phone Simon. That's all.'

'Look again. That's not me! I took a picture of her at Brent Cross and NOBODY ELSE COULD SEE HER.' I feel I'm shouting so I hush myself. 'It's true, Uncle Tom, not even Katie could see her but she was looking straight into my eyes, like she knew me, like she WAS me.'

Uncle Tom's eyes are telling me there's more to his story than he wants to share with Dad and Rosie Mum.

'Could it be Penelope? I think I've heard her voice,' I ask.

Uncle Tom's stare is even more intense.

'I'm not exactly sure but Stella was trying to tell me about a Penelope and a Philippa when she was slipping away. Perhaps you remember, Simon. I was asking her if those were the names she wanted for her twin girls but all she kept saying was no, no, no, the new twins had to be Poppy and Pippa. I don't think we need to worry about it though. Let's forget about it for the moment. Any chance I can stay for dinner, Rosie?'

'Sure, it'll be ready in half an hour,' she says and we all get back to reality land.

I slip my phone into my pocket and manage to get Uncle Tom to myself by asking him to come and see Stella's herb garden that I might clear. What's really weird is when I send the image to Uncle Tom's phone it comes out perfect. How the spook did that happen? He stares at the image and ums for a bit and shuts his eyes. After a while he speaks. 'It's not Pippa for sure; she wouldn't be dressed like that. Have you had any visits lately, Poppy, like someone telling you to do your hair that strange way?'

I can't stop catching my breath.

'How did you know that?' And out came the story of Voice telling me how to do the curly ringlets on Katie's head and how my fingers knew what to do all on their own.

'Ah. I think I know what's happened. Can we have a closer look? Ah yes, do you see her cheek?'

'I know, Uncle Tom, she's got my butterfly.'

'This must be Penelope. And Poppy, I didn't tell your Dad and Rosie everything Stella said. She was trying to tell me that Penelope and Philippa were coming again when the time was right but before she could tell me when, she had gone. Her last words were, "This time it WILL happen." I think I know what she meant. I've been guessing ever since and sometimes I hear her voice and some other voices too giving me clues.'

'What clues, Uncle Tom? Tell me please.'

'No, I can't. It might be dangerous to tell you in case I'm wrong. There's so much we don't understand out there - beyond the world we know. If you move away into the paranormal, normal people tend to say you're mentally ill. Just delete that picture and, if you can, try to forget that anyone or anything has been trying to contact you across the centuries.'

'Across the CENTURIES! What do you mean?'

'Sorry, Poppy. Please forget I said that. Perhaps I *am* crazy like the doctors say.'

'Don't say that.'

'And I wouldn't want you to be troubled like I've been over the years. Forget about this ghost, because that's what she is, and get on with your life in the real world. Ignore her and she'll go away.'

'But are you still hearing the voices, Uncle Tom?'

'Sometimes, but not so often now and Celia helps me.'

'How?'

'When they come she tells them to go away. She can't hear them, she says, but I sometimes wonder if they can hear her.'

'And do they go away?'

41

'Mostly.'

'I need to know because somebody is talking to me too.'

'I know.'

'That's scary, Uncle Tom. Do your voices talk about me?'

'Yes… Well, I think it's you. Oh, I don't know Poppy. I can't be sure. Forget I said that. Delete the picture.'

'No, I can't. I want to know more.' I can't help thinking I'm not getting the whole story from my strange uncle. We go inside for dinner.

'Well, what do you think Tom?' Dad asks.

'I think the picture should be deleted and we can all forget the whole thing but Poppy isn't so sure.'

Dad, what should I do?'

All this time, Dad and Rosie Mum have been looking scared and keeping quiet. Dad pushes his fingers through his hair and shakes his head.

'Perhaps you should listen to your uncle; it might save you a lot of heartache if you forget about all this nonsense.'

I need to get away so I run outside again and down to the old herb garden, gasping for breath.

'Rub me out and I'll come back,' Voice whispers and I want to scream but Mum is walking towards me calling my name so instead I hiss, 'Leave me alone. What do you want?'

'How can I leave you alone? I am you and you are me so you see it's impossible. But you can delete the picture to keep them happy but I'm in your cyberspace now forever.'

'Come back in, darling. You mustn't be alone now and try not to be scared.' Mum puts her arm around my shoulder and I find I'm crying with frustration but I'm no longer totally terrified. I know I'm talking to my own ghost and she means me no harm and I want to know more. Who says I'm not petrified?

I'm going to play along. I'll do what Uncle Tom says.

'Dad, delete your picture and I'm going to delete mine. Let's do it before I change my mind.' We make a little ceremony of killing off the other me and I quickly switch off my phone. Uncle Tom looks relieved.

'I'd better get home. Walk me to the car, Poppy.' When we're outside I get the chance to tell him what the voice said in the garden. Uncle Tom nods and looks grim. 'I'm even more sure this is Penelope and I think she's been reborn in you, but for now, don't scare your dad and Rosie or anyone. They won't understand. Stella didn't understand until just before she died and then she tried to explain it all to me but, to be honest, I'm not clear about what it all means.'

'Are you scared Uncle Tom?'

'I'm not sure. Sometimes I feel threatened but deep down, I don't feel they mean you any harm. Mostly, I feel as if I'm here to watch over you and … .'

'Me and who? What do your voices say, Uncle Tom?'

'Oh stuff like 'the time is getting closer' and 'your Poppy is learning how to be Penelope' and …um… something like 'Stella would be prood o' her wee herb wife'; I couldn't really make that bit out.'

'The voices said stuff like that to me too. And do they tell you about natural medicines?'

'No, never but then I'm not Penelope though I feel you are, or might be.'

'I can't be. That's impossible.'

'Yes you can. I think it's … oh, never mind. It's all too much to think about and if I'm wrong, you'll have been worried for nothing.'

'Tell me, please.'

'I can't. Not yet. For now, stay quiet about hearing the voices. I believe we, you and I, have a special gift but other people don't see it that way. They want to label us with some psychological condition or another; they don't understand what's out there in the paranormal.'

'You're cool Uncle Tom. I don't know what I'd do without our chats.'

'Go crazy, maybe?' he says with a twinkle in his eye. It feels so good to laugh after being spooked for what seems like forever. Maybe the ghosts aren't real after all. Then I remember the picture on my phone.

For a short time, life is back to normal. Ralph tumbles home after dinner at Charlie's and we chat as if nothing has happened.

Then, when it's time to go to bed and I'm safely in my room, I switch my phone back on!

Chapter 10:
Texts from the Past

My message alert whistles and I think it's Katie. It isn't. It's a picture message and some text. She's - or *I'm* - back, staring straight at the camera. Of course, it must be a copy of the image I sent to Dad. I won't delete it and they won't know, except Katie because I promised to tell her everything.

'here 2 stay.' the text reads.

I hit reply and type *'U said u'd come back and that u were me. How can that be?'*

'You'll find out soon enough.' I decide to save the mobile number and my blood runs cold. It's 31101 600 613 ; nobody's ever heard of a number like that. It's alien.

'What's your name?'

'Penelope – but you know that, don't you?'

'Who's Pippa?'

'Philippa, our twin.'

'OUR twin? Is she alive?'

'Yes and No. Goodbye.'

'Wait. I want to know more.'

'Not yet – but look at your picture gallery.'

When I open up my picture gallery there's a new folder so I click on it and find pages and pages of 'Penelope'. The message alert whistles:

'You don't have to count them; there are 400,' the text reads.

'Why?' There's no answer. I wait and wait but there's still no answer.

I'm trying to go to sleep but 400 pix of Penelope keep floating around my head. What have I done? She's punishing me for trying to kill her image. But she's me! And I can't be punishing myself – but oh yes, I can. On my bedside clock I see 1am, 2am, 3am and 4am before I unplug it and finally fall asleep so when 8:30am comes, I'm wrecked and Mum's voice next to my bed seems miles away.

'Are you coming into the shop with me, Poppy?'

'Not today, Mum, I need a long lie; I couldn't sleep.'

'I'm not surprised,' she says stroking my forehead while I whimper. 'That's fine, your dad's gardening so go back to sleep.'

I try but sleep won't come. I dial 31101 600 613. It's ringing. Oh my giddy ghost, it's real. The message comes back, *'Sorry, calls to this number are not being connected'* so I text, *'Why 400 pix?'*

'400 years since we began.'

'Began what?'

'You'll find the answer at the castle near the water.'

'What castle?'

'No more now until the castle.'

I ring Katie and she's about to go off to visit her grandparents overnight; she can't believe Cyber Spook can text and says she'll see me tomorrow but I could do with her company right now. Maybe I'll see what Dad's doing in the garden, but I won't tell him about Penelope's texts.

'It's looking good,' I tell Dad as he tips a big pile of weeds into the compost bin.

'Yep. It's just a quick mow before I attack that tangle of weeds at the bottom of the garden. I thought we could clear it and put a new patio for a barbecue and table and chairs. It's a great spot for catching the evening sun.

Something inside me lets out a silent scream and I want to shout, 'No o o o …,' at the top of my voice but Dad would be freaked out and start thinking what I now know; someone from

46

the past wants me to save the herbs. I take a deep breath and when I speak, I sound calm.

'Before you do that, I'd like to save some of the plants and put them in a special bed in the corner. Can I do that please?'

Dad gives me a strange look and nods quietly. 'I'll help you,' he says, 'but I don't know what's a weed and what isn't down there.'

'I do,' I say but wish I hadn't, as Dad nods again and looks miserable. It must be hard for him so I quickly add 'I've been looking them up in an encyclopedia I got in the library.'

'I suppose a weed is just a flower you didn't plant in the right place,' Dad says, looking wistful. 'Your mother used to say that.'

We understand each other and head down the garden past the tall hawthorn hedge which divides the old herb garden from the family garden of lawn, shrubs and flowers near the house. I begin by collecting boulders and stones which have been hidden under grass and weeds for years. Dad says he'd forgotten they were there. (I don't tell him I just knew they were there.) I choose two long patches along the wooden fence which meet at the far corner. Dad chooses a big square where he plans to put down patio blocks and outlines a path for stepping stones. We think the rest should be lawn and decide the hedge would look better trimmed well down. We decide to keep the juniper and mallow trees which have grown quite tall and straggly along the back fence; all they need is a trim.

'You can grind the juniper berries to rub on sore joints and make tea with mallow for coughs,' a voice says but it's not Penelope's voice this time. I feel strangely spurred on to action and full of energy all of a sudden.

I lay the stones in a row four feet away from the fence and round the corner. I find a big, old pot and fill it with compost from an unopened bag behind the shed. There aren't many plants in my new bed but I dig them out carefully and place

47

them in the pot of compost to keep them alive: bearberry (for urine problems), lily of the valley (for heart problems), cowslip (for the chest), adonis (for the nerves), coltsfoot (for rashes) and blueberry (for diarrhea).

How do I know all this stuff? This is creepy!

I can recognise the plants from their leaves and they'll soon have spring flowers. Then I start on clearing out the ground elder shoots, new because it's early spring. I'm planning to dig out the new bed and replant all the stuff from the rest of the herb garden

'Did you know bishop's weed is good for constipation?' the voice which isn't Penelope's asks.

'No, I'd forgotten,' I say. 'I thought this was ground elder.'

'Bishop's weed – same thing. And, please, get your father to wait until May before he clears out.

'Why?'

Many of the plants have to come up again after winter and if you don't wait, they will be destroyed. And you don't want to trim the hawthorn before the flowers and seeds come; you might need the berry juice to treat your own insomnia. Wait until May.'

'My own insomnia? What do you mean?' I say and wait for a reply that doesn't come.

I'll ask Dad to help me clear my new patch and plant out the saved plants and suggest we trim the juniper and mallow but not the hawthorn. Perhaps he'll be tired by then and won't mind waiting until May. I'm right.

We stop for lunch and again for tea. We don't go out after tea as the spring warmth dies away and it starts raining.

'I'll keep the weather bad now.'

'Can you do that?' I ask her.

'Watch me.'

For a while, life goes on the same boring old way and school is all about homework and revision. I don't even notice there are no cyber spooks or voices. I sometimes wonder if my dead twin and the person with the other voice can make me forget about them when I need to; perhaps they love me – not perhaps, I'm sure they do. Or am I sure?

Everyone's complaining about the coldest wettest March and April for years and by the time the May sun appears and the days get longer, the herb garden is full of new plants pushing their way up through the rough grass.

I'm amazed at the names which come to mind: yarrow (for bleeding gums), monkshood (for headaches and rheumatism), agrimony (for digestion), dill (for wind and to produce breast milk), anise (for stomach cramps), eyebright (for digestion and eye lotions), sundew (for breathing problems) and thyme (for wounds that won't heal).

How I know all this I'm not sure, but what I do know is that I must get out there and get them into my bed full of fresh compost, and save them. I'll start after school today now the end of year exams are over.

Katie wants to help and I tell her about the other voice and how I know all the names of the plants and what they are used for.

'Why am I not surprised anymore, Poppy? Still scared maybe, but not surprised.'

'Don't be scared. I feel loved,' I tell her. She rolls her eyes and then looks at me sideways.

We work steadily with a garden trowel, a kitchen spoon and a spade, digging and planting and watering until Mum calls us in for supper. The new bed is half full already and tomorrow's another day.

'Your mother would have been proud of you, Pops,' Dad tells me. 'She loved that garden.'

'I know.' It occurs to me that the other voice might be hers. 'You'll soon be able to build your patio and path. One more go at it and we should have transplanted all the herbs and flowers.

'I'll help tomorrow,' Dad says. 'It'll be great to get the barbecue area sorted.'

I can't believe how well the plants are flourishing in their new corner after just one day and with Dad, Katie and I working we clear the tangle and replant everything and water it in before too long. Why am I so happy about some stupid old plants? My heart's singing and I feel good. Katie and Dad are excited too, but more about planning the new patio set and barbecue. Mum will be happy as long as they aren't white plastic. 'It looks so grubby so quickly and it's horrible,' she says.

The weekend comes and the patio is soon laid with the help of Jim, Dad's builder friend. Ralph and I place the stepping stones all the way up to the house; Ralph hops all the way up and down for the rest of the day. Three days later the chosen garden furniture arrives: a hardwood table, four chairs, two sofas, green cushions and a green parasol to match. It looks amazing and Mum is delighted.

Katie for me and Charlie for Ralph are invited over for Sunday lunch and we drag the old barbecue down from the shed and cook some sausages and veggie burgers to go with seeded buns, green salad, mustard and caramelised onion chutney. Then the best bit is barbied marshmallows; yum.

While we drink some blackcurrant juice, Mum and Dad are enjoying a glass of red wine and I haven't seen them look so relaxed in a long time. I wonder if they think clearing the old garden has cleared out the old ghosts and sad memories. I hope so.

But I don't want the memories to fade and I feel responsible for the herb garden and desperately want to keep it going; I sense a presence again and this time it is comforting. This time, I will keep it a secret, even from Katie. Is there always one tiny bit of us that must stay a secret? I'm not sure, but I think so.

I've tried texting 31101 600 613 a couple of times but nothing comes back. There's something about that peculiar number that's familiar but I can't put my finger on it. I keep finding that last message:

'No more now – until the castle.'

The last days of summer term go by and Katie goes off to Canada, telling me I have to Skype her if there are any ghosts around. We've started packing for our cottage holiday near Loch Ness in the grounds of Ballindourie Castle. I love the name Heather Cottage.

Ralph has a new fishing rod and I'm taking a couple of Jacqueline Wilsons to read.

Before we go, Mrs. Jackson next door agrees to make sure the new herb garden is watered. That comforts me. I overhear Mum telling her how important that garden is to me.

'Unusual for such a young girl to love gardening so much,' I hear Mrs. Jackson almost whisper.

I can't wait to get to the castle.

Chapter 11:
Journey into the Unknown

'Give it a rest Ralph,' Dad's shouting as we speed up the M6 on the way to Scotland. Ralph has been giving us 'Greensleeves' on his recorder for 3 hours but I suppose he's getting better with practice.

'Yea,' I tell him. 'I'm getting a headache and I'm trying to read.'

'Okay,' he says, 'as long as I get to play 'Speed Bonny Boat' when we get to Gretna Green'.

'How do you know that one?' Mum asks.

'The music teacher's from Edinburgh and she says Greensleeves is the English song and Speed Bonny Boat is the Scottish song.'

'Well maybe a couple of times,' Dad says.

'But I have to practise. It makes perfect.'

'I suppose your teacher said that too,' sighs Mum.

All I can think of is that last text and what's waiting for us. Oh, why is this journey so long?

Motorways, motorways, motorways, cars, lorries and boring, boring scenery. It was almost better listening to Ralph's recorder. I wish he'd been allowed to use his PlayStation but Mum and Dad say we all need a break from technology to appreciate the scenery and the joys of nature. Our phones and Ralph's PlayStation are switched off and locked in the glove compartment. I blame it on Mum reading that book '*The Winter of Our Disconnect*'; now we have to have a summer of disconnect. Ralph isn't coping too well.

'When are we going to be there?' he whines and Mum and Dad laugh.

'I wondered how long it would take you to say that,' Dad says. 'If the whole journey is say 10 hours and we add some time for lunch, tea and petrol stops, how long would that be?'

'Maybe 12 hours?' Ralph says.

'We left at 8 o'clock,' I add, 'so we'll get there at 8 o'clock tonight.'

'I don't think I can sit in a car for that long, Mum,' says Ralph.

'We're due at the cottage tonight so we can't stop overnight,' Dad says.

I'm not sure I can stand Ralph bleating and fidgeting about in his seat belt.

'Ralph, why don't you read your *Captain Underpants*?' I tell him.

'It's in the boot! Can I read one of your books?'

I dig in my new, oversized, holiday handbag and bring out *Lily Alone*. I'm trying to read *The Worst Thing about my Sister* to take my mind off spooks.

'*Lily Alone*, yuk that's for girls; can I read that other one?'

'I'm reading this one.'

'Oh, please, Poppy.'

I know he'll soon get bored when he finds out it's for girls too so I let him have it and he settles down for a while. I'm happy just dreaming, imagining what's waiting for us at the castle. I shut my eyes and pretend to sleep. I'm itching to check my messages and I keep seeing *No more now – until the castle* in my head. WHO was texting and HOW did we get to hear about the cottage in the castle grounds? WHAT is waiting for us there and WHY?

'When are we stopping for lunch?' complains Ralph. 'Poppy, this book's boring.'

'Come on then, let's play I spy,' I say.

But that's for little kids!' says Ralph.

'I'd like to play,' says Dad, so we play, because Ralph idolises Dad.

'I've got a good one,' says Mum. 'I spy with my little eye something beginning with S?' (I want to say spooks but I don't.)

'Sky.' 'Seatbelt.' 'Socks' 'Give up.'

'Skoda car,' says Mum. 'Gotcha. My turn again.'

'No, my turn,' says Ralph.

'Oh all right,' Mum says and we play on for a while until we reach a motorway service station.

'Oh, look, cowboys!' Ralph shouts pointing at six life-size wooden statues with their guns in their holsters. 'Can I go and touch them?'

A dad with his son on his shoulders comes by, drawling like an American. 'Do you know what they're saying? "This service station ain't big enough for the six of us".'

'Wicked,' says Ralph, bending his head back to look up at the craggy, wooden faces.

McDonalds wins out over Costa and Greggs. 'Just for once', Mum says, but I think she's enjoying her Mayo Chicken, Garden side salad and fries.

'I'll need some dessert,' Ralph whines.

'Oh, there's no time if we want to get there tonight,' I say, my heart sinking.

'Fine, you're on holiday,' Dad says, so we *all* have a gooey treat; mine's a Galaxy McFlurry with chocolate - and a million calories. Who cares?

'Are we near Scotland yet?' Ralph asks.

'About 100 miles.'

'I need my *Captain Underpants* from the boot then.'

'Your what?'

'It's a book, Dad,' I say. I daren't ask for my phone though I'm dying to check for a text. What if there's no signal in the wilds of Scotland?

'Why did we ever think you kids would be happy enjoying the scenery?' Mum says as Ralph and I pick up a pack of playing cards and travel *Guess Who* at WH Smith's. We stop off at the 5 star loos with air con and travel toothpaste in a £1 chewball from a machine. Mum reckons everything's a ruddy rip off. I'm just impatient! I can't wait to get to the castle.

Back in the car Ralph and I start a game of *Guess Who* while Mum and Dad listen to oldie music on the radio.

We play 3 games of seven-card rummy and then we hit a bit of the journey like a moon land with a windy road through steep hills and little valleys with streams tumbling down to somewhere I can't see. This is totally another world, away from streets and cars and sirens in the distance, telling you something bad has happened.

'Hey, this is so cool,' says Ralph, and for once I agree with him.

'We're in the Lake District,' Dad tells us.

'How come we've never been to the Lake District or Scotland but we've been to Spain and Greece and Disneyland and Fuerteventura and Southend?' Ralph says counting on his fingers.

'Not sure, Ralphy' says Dad, 'but maybe it's because we think we're not on holiday unless we get on a plane.'

'Is Scotland like this?' Ralph asks.

'Even better,' Mum says and I know she's right because I can see pictures in my head of mountains and lochs with reflections of more mountains and I can smell fresh air and hear nothing but the sound of waves on a loch side and the call of birds high up in the sky. Are these pictures real?

'Where does all that water go from the streams?' Ralph asks.

'Well some of the streams flow into bigger rivers which flow into lakes or the sea,' Dad tells him, 'just like they have done for millions of years.'

'And for many millions more,' a familiar husky voice whispers.

'Did you hear that, Ralph?' I ask.

'Hear what?' he asks. So that was a no then. My stomach turns over.

'Ooh, I can see a big river running beside us,' Ralph says and before long we're on a bridge crossing over it.

'Ooh, it's on the other side of the road now,' Ralph shouts. He's getting excited. I would be too because when do we ever get away from streets and cars at home? But I feel sick with anxiety. This spooky stuff is getting really real.

'Is it our fault our kids have missed out on the beauties of our home country?' Mum asks.

'Perhaps it is,' Dad replies. 'But we'll make up for that this time.'

I wish I had my phone! I feel cut off from my future!

'You don't need your phone to get to your future but you must visit your past first.'

Was that Penelope or the other voice? My palms are sweaty and I'm wondering how she can read my thoughts. But of course, she's me!! But I can't see her.

'Hey, kids, do you want to see where some of these rivers go?' Dad shouts. 'My driving brain's tired.' Oh no, not another delay? He heads off the motorway and we follow the signs for Ullswater. I'm getting really cross now. Why don't they understand how anxious I am to get to the castle?

'Rosie, do you remember Pooley Bridge?'

'Of course, I do! We came here one Easter when Poppy went on holiday with Katie to Cornwall.'

'Was I born?' asked Ralph.

'No, you were born in the January of the following year.' I smile as I count the months off on my fingers. Dad and Mum are chuckling but Ralph is staring out of the window, mesmerized by the scenery in the sunshine.

56

'Where do these rivers go? I can't see.'

After a while, we pull up near the shores of the most beautiful lake I think I've ever seen but it's not the lake in my imagination. There's no castle and the trees are roundy not pointy. There are grassy hills and woods all around and a boat with a red funnel is chugging across the water.

Wow. Can we come and live here?' Ralph asks.

'You wish,' I say. 'What's this lake called?'

'It's the famous Coniston Water.' Mum tells us. We cross a little bridge over a river and we have a chat about whether the river is coming in or going out of the lake.

'It's going out,' Dad says. 'Look how the water is flowing.'

'Come on, it's time to go,' I almost shout.

'All right Pops,' Dad snaps. 'I just need to stretch my legs. Why can't you just enjoy this beautiful place?'

'Sorry,' I say, feeling guilty about making Dad feel bad.

We go for a little walk and at last Dad's ready to tackle the last bit of the journey but the stupid car isn't. It won't start. Oh no.

'I'll ring the AA if you get my phone out,' I say quickly, spotting an opportunity. Dad digs his AA card out of his wallet while Mum unlocks the glove compartment. I pretend there's no reception while I check for Cyber Spook. Nothing.

Dad finally rings and the AA man arrives within half an hour but the car needs a part which won't arrive for two hours. Mum says we should call the castle to tell them we'll come tomorrow and Ralph is thrilled because he wants to go on a boat. I want to cry.

We use my smartphone to check for cancellations but there aren't any. The AA man, however, finds the last family room in a hotel run by his sister.

'It's not the best room,' he says, 'but it's nearby and I'll tow you there and get the part delivered.' Dad tells him he is a very, very, very nice man and Mum, Dad and he are laughing a lot. I can't see what's so funny and neither can Ralph. I suppose it's quite exciting to be towed. The hotel looks a bit old and tired but we're in time for afternoon tea with sandwiches, cakes and biscuits on one of those three plates high things. A young Aussie waitress tells us she's called Kelly, not Kylie, and she's on a gap year here.

'You could catch the Swallows and Amazons cruise at 4:30 from next to the Bluebird Cafe,' she tells us. 'You'll see Wild Cat Island.'

We get there in time and there's a song playing in the café about Donald Campbell drowning and I'm feeling like jelly as I can see his face floating above me. His ghost must be restless – and how the limbo do I know that?

'What's that tune?' I ask but I'm just checking because I know it's called 'Out of this World' by Marillion but I don't know how I know. Am I out of this world? Am I a ghost?

We pile on to the steamer and sit on wooden benches near the front. Then Ralph and I run to the back and watch the white foam stretching out behind us and sniff the air that's sweeter than ever it was in North London. Mum and Dad look so happy huddled together on a bench, looking around at the lake and the hills beyond. Ralph gets chatting to two boys who are excited about going kayaking tomorrow; they are asking him if he wants to come and he's telling them he's going to a haunted castle in Scotland, and the boys look dead jealous which is what Ralph wants.

I talk to a lady with white hair, staring eyes and a big smile. She tells me William Wordsworth and his sister Dorothy used to come here on holiday and this is where he wrote his most famous poem 'Daffodils'. I tell her I read it at school and I like it. She stares at me again.

'Have you got the sight?'

'Yes, I think I have,' I say without thinking.

'Well, my dear, I hope it is a blessing, not a curse. Stay well.'

'Oh look,' Mum calls as we pass a little island in the middle of the lake. 'There's a late little brood of cygnets.' I think this is the best bit of the trip so far; these baby swans are so cute. But the old lady's words are haunting me.

The old lady asks Ralph if he knows who Mr Whoppit is but he doesn't so she tells him. 'He's the teddy bear who broke the world water speed record in a boat called the Bluebird.'

'A teddy bear couldn't do that,' Ralph protests.

'He could if he went with his skipper Sir Donald Campbell,' Dad says.

Ralph loves the story of how the teddy bear mascot floated to the surface of the water but the Bluebird and Donald Campbell stayed down and weren't found for years. They're selling Mr Whoppit teddies in the tourist shop but Ralph reckons he's a bit too old for one of those so Dad buys him a picture of Mr Whoppit on a boat. Sometimes my little brother is quite cute.

I'm really desperate to get to my fairy castle but I'm glad we came here, especially since it's where Ralph started. What a strange thought.

The car has been fixed by the time we get back to the hotel so we'll be able to leave in the morning. Well, thank goodness for that.

Ralph and I are so tired after dinner we don't care that we have to share a lumpy sofa bed in Mum and Dad's room.

In my dreams Voice calls out: *'not long now'*… and I wake up dying to check my phone but Mum has locked it away again.

'Mum, how long do we have to have our time of disconnect?' I ask during breakfast, and I know I'm whining. I'm looking at a blackboard with a white chalk message, not a menu but: **Sorry No Wi-Fi. Speak to each other** – Mum says she likes it. Huh.

'A bit longer, Poppy. Live in the moment.' So I'm trying and I even eat porridge without moaning before we pile back into the car.

The countryside is rushing by and the clouds are making shadows on the hillsides. After a few miles we come out of the hills and I can see a city in the distance. Then there's more countryside with the sea on the left. The clouds become darker.

Chapter 12:
Welcome to Scotland

'Scotland's coming,' Dad shouts, 'and so's the rain', he adds making Mum laugh.

'Where?' Ralph mumbles sleepily.

'Watch out for the "Welcome to Scotland" sign,' Dad says.

After a while Ralph and I shout out, 'There it is' and while Ralph looks for his recorder to bug us with "Speed Bonny Boat", the rain starts to chuck down and we all laugh. Mum tells us the story of Gretna Green, how girls and boys can run away at sixteen and get married without their parents' permission.

'I thought boys could get married at 14 and girls at 12,' I say loudly but I don't know where that came from.

'That might have been true hundreds of years ago or in other parts of the world but not in the UK now,' Mum says.

'You are right Poppy, but so is your stepmother. Your first mother married young.' This is the first man's voice I've heard.

'My first mother?' I hiss almost silently. 'What do you mean? How young?'

'Thirteen. But she lost two babies before she had you twins. That's why she was so devastated to lose you.'

I dare not ask any more questions. I don't want Mum, Dad and Ralph to hear anything. How did she lose me I wonder?

'But it's just like England,' Ralph says as we look out over a big sign for Gretna Green Outlet Village. I hope we're not going shopping and thank goodness Dad drives on quickly into Gretna Green.

'I hope the Blacksmith's shop is still around; it's years since I was here, Simon, before we got married when…'

'I was still married to Stella, you mean.'

'Uhuh,' Rosie replies sheepishly but Dad smiles and tells her it's okay.

'Oh look, a piper in a kilt,' I shout. 'Ooh and there's a bride arriving in a white dress and a veil. But she's not 16, she's old.'

'At least twenty five, I'd say,' Dad adds. He and Mum laugh.

'I think it's just a fun and fashionable place to get married these days, never mind how old you are,' Mum says.

Ralph wants to ask the piper how he makes the noise. The piper's pleased to be asked but I'm not sure how much Ralph understood. I *think* this is what he said.

'Weel, laddie, ye fill the bag wi the bellows or if ye've got the win, ye blaw until it fills, and then it canna get oot until ye let it. Then ye have to keep blawin and letting oot fin ye're playin.'

'Right,' Ralph says in a slow and quiet voice. 'Thanks.' Then I think he has decided not to ask any more questions except he changes his mind.

'Can you play "Speed Bonny Boat"?'

'I can that! I call it "The Skye Boat Song "; I might have time to play it for ye before these waddins kick off. Would ye like that?'

Ralph nods and when the piper has played one verse as quietly as possible on bagpipes Ralph says, 'I can play that on my recorder.'

'Good for you. Do you see this bit at the bottom of my pipes? I could take it off the bag and play it like a recorder. It's called a chanter.'

'Dad, do you think I could get some bagpipes?'

I think it is 'Heaven forbid' that Mum says with her hand on her cheek.

'Not today, Ralph, but thank you sir for answering my son's question.'

'My pleasure,' says the piper whose name we'll never find out as he has to start playing for the wedding party – some lively tune I know from some distant past, but not the name. Isn't that annoying – and a bit frightening?

We've got time for a quick look around the original marriage room in the famous blacksmith's shop, where we see the anvil where the weddings took place, before we head back to the motorway. It doesn't look much like castle-country here. There are cars and lorries and horrible buildings everywhere. I didn't think Scotland was like this.

'What's the matter, Pops?'

'Scotland's no different.' I keep quiet though I'm so scared my dream is going to vanish.

'Wait until we get past Glasgow on the road to Loch Lomond. You'll definitely see the difference there,' says Dad.

'I'm going to shut my eyes until we get to a pretty part,' I say and I try, but I can't because I don't want to miss anything.

Glasgow comes and goes and eventually we find ourselves on a quieter road which looks more interesting until we find ourselves behind a caravan that's going so slowly that Dad's getting annoyed, but not as much as I am. I want to do a Ralph and ask when we're going to be there. Luckily the road widens and we can get past before it gets narrow again.

When we reach Loch Lomond, it's so beautiful I know why there are songs about it but we're stuck behind another caravan and the road is winding round steep rocks on the left and the loch on the right. I can't help looking at the green islands in the middle of the shiny, blue, smooth loch. I'm fidgeting, I know and Dad's cross.

'Just relax. We don't have a plane to catch,' Mum says.

'It's okay for you,' says Dad, 'but I have to really concentrate.'

'Why can't I read the signs now?' Ralph asks and Mum tells him they're written in Gaelic. Dad grumbles that they should have spent the money on the flipping road, not the signs. He must be getting tired.

We stop to stretch our legs and it's wonderful. I feel as if somebody has opened a door out to the world away from the city.

'I love this place,' I say. I don't say I feel as if I'm going home but I really do and I don't know why and I don't want to upset anyone by saying that.

Mum takes over the driving and Dad looks around.

We've left Loch Lomond behind and we can see Ben Nevis, the highest mountain in Britain and Glencoe, where the Campbells massacred their hosts the Macdonalds under the orders of King William II. Dad is keeping us informed.

'I don't like this bit; it's evil looking,' Ralph says as we are driving through Glencoe with the steep hills on both sides, blotting out the sun. I'm imagining the screaming of the Macdonalds running away from the Campbells.

'Hey, this bit looks like Hagrid's place in Harry Potter,' I suggest.

'I think it is,' says Dad, 'and the filmmakers used it in James Bond's Skyfall too.' How does my father know all these things?'

Now we're coming to another loch and people are water skiing.

'Ooh, this place is so pretty. How do you say B a l a c h u l i s h?' I say, spelling it out.

'Balahoolish,' Mum says. It looks more like my dream but there isn't a castle in sight.

'I don't know about you lot, but I need a cup of tea,' Mum says as we park near a roadside café.

'Can I have an ice cream?' Ralph asks.

'We might as well have lunch,' Dad suggests so we all have giant sausage rolls and tea and yummy chocolate squares.'

'We've reached the Caledonian Canal now,' Dad says back in the driving seat. All this wonderful scenery is fine but I'm getting *so* totally impatient now.

'Loch Ness!' Mum shouts. 'And there's a crannog.'

'What's that?'

'It's an island which people built to live safely on, hundreds of years ago,' I say BUT I DON'T KNOW HOW I KNOW THAT.

'That's right Pops; you've been doing your research.' I won't tell Dad I *so* have *not.*'

We get on to a really small road that Sat Naff wants us to take. All I can think of is getting to the castle to find out what's next with cyber spook! Why is this journey so *slow*?

'Oh no, not a B road Sat Naff!' Dad says. 'I think we'll take the A82 to Inverness and then come back down to the castle. At least we'll see the Loch all the way and keep moving. Watch out for the Loch Ness monster kids!'

Ralph is looking everywhere for Nessie but I've got cantbebotheredness. I *need* my phone.

'Stop Dad; there's Nessie,' says Ralph so we stop but it's a boat and we laugh. That's when I see that castle; it's a ruin but I don't know when or why.

'Oh no, what's happened to the castle? They've just finished doing it up.'

'Really?' Mum said.

The Grants fixed the broken walls; we came to see it.' I think I spoke out loud.

'No, Pops. That's Urquhart Castle and it's been a ruin for hundreds of years. It's a visitor centre now.'

I'm feeling cold and outside my mind, hovering between the past and the future. I shut my eyes and see the castle, whole and beautiful, with cows on the grass near the loch. I'm in a

65

garden picking greenery to put in a basket. I can't see who's with me but I'm not alone. I'm shaking.

I can hear Ralph in the distance. 'She's doing that on another planet thing, Mum.' The next thing Mum's in the back seat holding me and I can see Dad with his head down on the steering wheel. The picture of the castle in its glory is still in my head but something tells me not to share the memory.

'Sorry. I made a mistake. I've never been there. Dad it's ok. Sorry.' I wonder if my dead mother used to see things and scare him. I want to hug him but he has already started the car.

Dad's been driving too quickly now for a while and nobody is speaking. In the distance on the other side of the loch, peeping out from woodland, I see my fairy castle, all turrets and spires and crenellations – I know every room and every corner of the garden and every inch of the path through the woods down to the water's edge and the best place to sit silently and wait for the deer to come. This time I'll guard my secret memory. I know why Uncle Tom said, 'We have a gift, Poppy but most people will never understand that.'

'Welcome Home Penelope; I have someone to introduce you to before the sun goes down over the loch.' I think that was the woman's voice.

I screw my eyes shut, pretending to sleep and hug my elbows with my hands to stop my body shaking. I want to shout, 'My name's not Penelope,' again but I don't.

'She's asleep,' I hear Mum whisper. 'Don't worry, Simon, she's just a bit fey.'

We drive north to Inverness, cross a bridge and head south again to Ballindourie and when we get there, it's the castle I saw and I *do* know every corner.

'We have to pick up the cottage keys from the office,' Mum says fishing through a file of papers. We follow the signs to the Main Office, a building at the back, and I'm feeling more this worldly when I see the castle gardens are completely different

66

and the building has new windows and painted doors. Can it still be enchanted?

Dad goes into the office for the keys and comes back to say we can park near the office and walk to the cottage in the wood if we have wheelie suitcases.

A teenage boy comes out of the office and offers to show us the way, until...

'Aye aye, Pippa,' he says to me. 'Do ye ken these folk? Maybe ye can show them the wye to Heather Cottage. The golfers have just got back and you ken fit that means.'

Chapter 13: Pippa

The boy runs off, to look after the golfers I suppose, before we can lift our jaws up.

'Pippa?' says Ralph.

`C'mon,' I say shrugging my shoulders, 'There's the sign to Heather Cottage.' We follow the path which is wider than I remember but I *know* what we'll find at the end of it. We're led to the water's edge where a giant old tree is dipping the tips of its branches into the loch. The path then turns back away from the loch and up a short hill towards 'Heather Cottage' with its white walls and apple green window frames and front door.

'Up the brae awa fae the floods,' the deeper voice I sometimes hear says.

'It's lovely,' Mum cries and Dad and Ralph are grinning. I'm puzzled; it is, and yet it isn't, a cottage I remember from somewhere, sometime, a long time ago.

'Bags I have a bedroom where I can look for the monster,' Ralph says eyeing the two upstairs windows on either side of the big door in the middle and above the two big downstairs windows. The view over Loch Ness is *amazing.*'

'Isn't this lovely? Flowers on the table and a bottle of red wine. Sorry kids, not for you,' Mum says.

But we look in the fridge to find cans of Irn-Bru, milk, butter, bread, raspberry jam, ice cream in the freezer section and four big, high scones with cream and jam.

'Tea,' says Mum filling the kettle. 'I always feel a place is home after I've boiled the kettle.' Tea, coffee, cocoa and sugar are all there. There's even instant porridge and a squeezy bottle of honey.

'They've thought of everything,' Dad says.

After the best scones and tea in the world we sit in the bay window watching the sun slipping down behind the trees on the hills on the other side of the loch. I know what's going to happen next. This must be the 'gift'. The doorbell rings and Mum goes to the door. I wait for her scream. It comes and Dad rushes out.

'I'm sorry,' we hear him say to the person at the door. 'Come in and you'll see why she got a shock.'

Next moment, my double walks in. Incredibly, neither of us seems surprised.

'You must be Pippa,' I say. 'I used to call you that when I was little.'

'And you must be Poppy,' she says.

'Yes, I'm Poppy.'

'Ministry of the bleedin obvious,' my twin barks. We're very different in some ways.

There seem to be a lot of unanswered questions but here and now is not the time to get the answers. Dad is doing that pushing his hands through his hair thing and there's a stunned silence. Ralph's open mouth is catching flies. After what seems like ages, Mum finally speaks.

'Why don't you two go for a walk and get to know each other?'

. . .

'This is amazing,' Pippa says. 'I only came to drop off anither bottle o' milk. My mam's in charge o' servicing the cottages.'

We set off along the edge of the loch until we find a low branch to sit on and watch tiny waves hitting a mini sandy beach. We've been stealing glances at each other for the past few minutes.

'Did you know you had a twin?' I ask. I can't help noticing that she doesn't have a birthmark on her cheek.

69

'Yes, my adoptive parents told me. We're nae really identical,' she says. 'You've got a birthmark.'

'Did you know our mother had died?'

'Aye.'

'I thought you had died too.'

'Did they tell ye that?'

'I'm not sure. I think so or maybe they said you'd gone and I thought they meant dead. Our dad gets upset when we talk about it.'

'*Our* dad... oh aye he must be.' I've decided I like Pippa's lilting Scots accent.

After a while of us just staring at each other, Pippa asks, 'Did ye ken our mother?'

'No, she died when we were born, but I sometimes think she's still around.'

'Me an aw, and I kent ye were comin.'

'How?' I ask though I think I know.

'Because of the voices.'

'You hear the voices too.

'Aye but I've niver telt onybody. They might think I was glaikit.'

'What's glaikit?'

'Stupid. Wrong in the head.'

'Are you scared?'

'Naw, I'm nae feart usually but it gave me a fleg when I saw ye first.'

'What?'

'Sorry I forget you're English; ye seem jist like me. I'm nae feart means I'm not frightened and a fleg's a fright.'

'I'm not feart either,' I say trying to copy Pippa and we both fall about laughing like we've been friends forever.

'What I want to find out is why our father made me think you were dead, Pippa.'

70

'Okay, shall we go and ask him?' Pippa says in her poshest English accent.

When we get back to the cottage we find Dad alone and he tells us Mum and Ralph have gone to buy some dinner in the village shop.

'Dad, what happened? Pippa really is my twin, isn't she and you're her dad, aren't you?'

He does this 'hands through the hair' bit for a while and then begins to speak.

'I can't believe this has happened. I was trying to do the best for both of you. When Stella died, I fell to pieces and I didn't know how to cope with one baby, far less two. There were no grandparents around with Stella your mum's parents in Australia and my parents dead, (Granny is Rosie's mum Poppy) and only Tom, your uncle, was there so when the social worker suggested I put you up for adoption, it sounded like an answer but then I just couldn't give you both up. There was a couple, they told me, who wanted a baby but couldn't cope with twins. I had no idea who they were or where they lived; that was how I wanted it. I couldn't choose which of you to keep so they made the decision for me, to have one of you adopted, and it was you Pippa (that's what Stella wanted to call you).

'Why?' Pippa asks, close to tears.

'They said you would be less vulnerable because you didn't have a birthmark. When you were tiny Poppy, your birthmark was bright red and prominent, though it's faded now, but I loved you all the same though I wasn't sure if someone else would.'

'Why couldn't you have kept us together?' I say, tears welling up.

'Do you think I haven't thought about that every day for all the years since you grew out of being tiny babies totally dependent on me? I should have found a nanny but there wasn't much money around.'

'Could Rosie Mum not have helped out?'

'I hardly knew her except as your mum's colleague so I thought I couldn't ask her ... but if I'd known we were going to get married later, I would have. Then there was Tom. He kept saying Stella wanted the twins to be separated which didn't make any sense and it still doesn't.'

Pippa and I look at each other and this time, there *is* fear in both our eyes. We'll discuss this when we are next alone.

'Girls, I'm so, very, very sorry. I loved you both and I still do. Come here.' He holds out his arms wide and we both go into them and wait until his sad chest stops heaving and he finally lets go.

'It must have been very hard,' Pippa says taking the words out of my mouth. I think she must have been born first.

'Dad, who's older?' I ask.

'You, Pippa, by twenty minutes.'

'Listen, I'll need to get home for my tea but we'll get together tomorrow. Please can I talk to my mum and dad before you meet them? They're in for a bit of a shock.'

'I'll walk half way with you,' I say. 'Dad, I'll be back in a minute.' We leave him opening one of the two beers Pippa's mum had left in the fridge. He'll need it.

Our words tumble out together as we rush to get answers to our questions.

Yes, we'd both seen our double, yes, we'd both heard voices, two not just one, yes she knew a bit about herbal medicine, no, she couldn't put ringlets in hair, no, I didn't know how to skin a swan, no, she hadn't got any texts but yes she'd got messages written on a steamy mirror.

'Oh no, my phone's locked in the glove compartment and I want to show you the photograph of the other me.'

'You've got a photo?'

'Yes – 400 copies for 400 years, the texts said.'

'400 years! What does that mean?'

'It scares me to think about it,' I say.

'I know why I didn't get the texts; the reception's rubbish around here. Ye can get it but ye have to climb the hill a bit at the back of your cottage.'

'Oh, oh. Look who's coming.' Rosie Mum, Ralph and what looks like Pippa's adoptive parents are walking along the path towards us.

'Well, now fancy this,' Pippa's mum says looking from one to the other of us. 'I'm Caitlin Drummond, Pippa's mum.' She looks a bit miffed.

'Poppy Danford,' I say shaking the hand she offers me.

'I'm Rory, her Dad,' and I shake his hand too. It's all a bit formal but it makes things easier.

'I see you've met my step mum and step brother,' I say. 'Pippa, this is Rosie and Ralph.'

'Hi Pippa,' Rosie says. 'I feel as if I know you; you were Poppy's imaginary friend until she was about four.'

Caitlin says, 'We wanted to call her Philippa but ... .'

'I'm *not* Philippa!' Pippa says just like I sometimes say, 'I'm *not* Penelope'.

'She used to call you Pippa,' Rory adds, 'when you were *her* imaginary friend.'

'Pippa, Robbie's fair got the heebie-jeebies,' Caitlin interrupts, still tetchy. 'First he sees you goin doon the road and then ye're in the back office.'

'Poor Robbie,' says Pippa, pulling a face.

Caitlin keeps on. 'What I want to know is how you found us. We were told this couldn't happen.'

Rosie's in a panic. 'I honestly don't know how we found you but please, can we talk to Simon, the girls' father first? He's desperately upset about this whole situation.'

We find Dad standing in the bay window looking out over the loch looking glum. After some more handshaking and silent nodding he speaks first.

'I don't know how we landed here.'

'We know how,' Pippa and I say in one voice. 'Nobody else does,' we say, again together. We're definitely twins with a mental connection.

'One at a time. Poppy, you first. How do you know?'

'It's something supernatural – a spirit.' I say, shaking my head the tiniest bit so Pippa can see but nobody else. She keeps quiet too about who it might be.

'What? I've never heard anything so daft.' Caitlin says.

'Mam, I think she's right. I hav'nae been telling you but I've been hearing voices for a year now, since my last birthday. I knew Poppy was coming. I got messages on the mirror in the bathroom too. They were saying, "Poppy misses Pippa", and, "She's coming soon"'.

'Why didn't you tell us?' Caitlin adds raising her voice. Rory finally speaks.

'Don't you remember, Caitlin, when we were told the baby was called Pippa you wanted to change it to Philippa to wipe out the past? Then when she started speaking to Poppy, she told us her name had to be Pippa.'

'I do remember that. I just wanted to feel, after all the years without a baby, that this little girl was really ours – and now…' Caitlin turns away and I think she's hiding tears.

'Dinna greet Mam, I'll aye be your daughter and you're the best mam I could ever have.' My face is hurting so much with trying to stop crying and I see Rosie wiping her eyes so I hug her while Pippa hugs Caitlin.

'Is this a disaster or can we sort it?' Rory says.

'Who's going to stay where now?' Ralph asks. Why do kids always manage to come out with what everyone else dare not say?

Dad is quick to react. 'When the holiday's over, we go home and carry on as usual.' Maybe, but we all know that things are never going to be the same. I'm looking over at Pippa and I know she's thinking what I'm thinking; twins should be together.

'Dad, can I borrow the car keys? I think everybody needs to see that picture.'

Rory and Caitlin look puzzled but Pippa looks excited. 'I'll come with you to the car. I can't wait to see this.'

As we're walking along the path with the setting sun peeping through the trees, I know I've been here before.

'Have you got déjà vu?' Pippa lilts.

'Definitely have.' We join hands and run to the car.

'Damn,' I say after wrestling with the keys and getting the phone out. 'The barking battery's dead.' I fish the charger out and Ralph's PlayStation while I'm at it and we run back down to the cottage where the four parents (four!) are drinking red wine and Ralph is having Irn Bru. I start charging my smartphone before Pippa and I dive into the big bowlful of crisps. There isn't enough charge to show the pic. We all sit around the little round table in the bay window looking out over the loch and the furious crunching of crisps is relieved by Ralph's silly comments about seeing the monster.

'Where did you see your other you?' I ask Pippa and watch the shock spread over her parents' face.

'M&S in Inverness but I didn't take a picture.'

My phone charges enough to show the pic to Pippa. 'That's not me; that's you. Look at the birthmark. I always thought we were seeing each other but …'

'Didn't you think she was you when you saw her?' I ask.

'I didn't have time to think about it and I really didn't want anyone to think I had a loose screw, so I pretended I hadn't seen her.'

The others are looking at the picture.

'But we watched you delete that,' Dad yells.

'I did but she or...something... sent it again and ... ,' I say but stop myself from adding 400 times. Caitlin and Rory are double flabbergasted, Ralph is super excited and Rosie's in a panic.

'But that's not you,' Ralph is saying. 'Could it be your ghost?' Again, he's speaking the unspeakable. 'Look at the clothes and the hair.'

I decide I'd better tell everyone about Cyber Spook; I can't keep it a secret any more. I show them the whole conversation thread:

'here 2 stay.'

'u said u'd come back and that u were me. How can that be?'

'You'll find out soon enough.'

'What's your name?'

'Penelope – but you know that, don't you?'

'Who's Pippa?'

'Philippa, our twin.'

'OUR twin. Is she alive?'

'Yes and No. Goodbye.'

'Wait. I want to know more.'

'Not yet – but look at your picture gallery.'

'You don't have to count them; there are 400.'

'Why?'

'400 years since we began.'

'Began what?'

'You'll find the answer at the castle near the water.'

'What castle?'

'No more now – until the castle.'

So the texts are from Penelope and her odd phone number is 31101 600 613

'Dial it!' Pippa shouts. 'Hang on. There's something about that number ringing bells.'

76

'I would if there was any service,' I reply. 'Come on; let's go up to the top of the hill.'

Everyone has to come of course and before we all traipse to the top, my phone goes mental, whistling in texts, missed calls, Facebook posts and WhatsApp messages.

'That's what happens when you want a time of disconnect,' I say to Rosie Mum. 'Now I don't know where to start.'

'Dial Penelope's number,' shouts Pippa.

'*Sorry, calls to this number are not being connected.*'

I start texting before Pippa tells me to; we're twins after all.

'*Penelope, we've met at the castle. What did we begin 400 years ago?*' We wait for a while, and wait some more. Eventually a reply comes:

'*Wait until u 2 are alone.*' I hide the message from everyone else and flash it near Pippa before checking my other messages.

Katie wants to know if Cyber Spook has made contact and says hello to everyone. Canada's all about weddings she says. Loads of randoms are sending silly messages on Facebook and there are some holiday pics on WhatsApp from various school friends.

'Nothing from Penelope?' Pippa asks

'Nothing,' I say. 'Why don't you all go back and we'll come down later,' I suggest to the four parents and Ralph. They reckon that's a good idea so I send another text:

'*We're alone now.*'

'*Estelle wants you to be together.*'

'*Who's Estelle?*'

'*Our mother, of course but she was Stella by the time she gave birth to you two.*'

'*We don't know what you mean.*'

'*You will understand soon. Pippa, send me a text from your phone. Philippa and I have not been able to communicate well with you. We have to tell you both something important.*'

'Pippa's phone is at home. She'll text later.'

'Pippa and Poppy, you must decide how much to tell your families. Not everyone can move between parallel worlds.'

'You mean Pippa and I can?'

'Yes but you must take care; this is the 4th time we've tried and we don't want to fail again. Cyberspace has helped a lot this time so we feel hopeful. For now, goodbye.'

I tell Pippa there's no point in going on after one of these goodbyes so we head down to the cottage with our heads full of questions.

'Well?' says Ralph when we get back.

'Somebody calling herself Penelope says somebody called Estelle wants the two of us to be together.'

'Who the cyber spook is Estelle?' Ralph asks.

We twins don't have to tell each other to stay quiet. My dad has gone as white as a sheet and I suspect he knows but he's keeping very quiet.

'Look, I think we're all exhausted and it's time we had dinner so let's call it a day,' says Dad.

'Yes, let's see what tomorrow brings,' adds Rory who seems to be the calmest person around.

Pippa borrows a pen and paper to write down that peculiar phone number.

'I'm supposed to text this number so Poppy and I can find out something important.'

There's no way, Pippa,' Caitlin says, 'that you're goin up that brae again the nicht. Do you hear me?'

'Okay, Mam but can I go upstairs to the top of the castle? They won't mind if we say it's an emergency.'

'It's just a bunch of fanciful havers; you can't call it an emergency,' Rory says, very, very quietly, like he's not really sure. 'But I suppose we're not going to get any sleep if you don't find out what's going on. It's just some kind of scam, I'm sure. You'd better settle in and have your meal. We'll phone down on the landline if we find out anything interesting. Come Pippa, home.'

None of us feel like scrambled eggs on toast, the most exciting thing in the village shop, but we eat it; we're alone and there's one question hanging in the air. Where did that brochure with the red circle round Ballindourie Castle appear from? I have a good idea who planted it there but how, I have no idea.

I get Dad alone. 'What scares you so much about the name Estelle?'

'I wasn't going to tell you this.' He shoves his hand through his hair again. 'When your mother was pregnant she used to shout out...'

'Yes?'

'Things like, "No, Estelle, I can't let you in", or, "Leave me alone Estelle", or other stuff. Then when you were born, she seemed to be speaking to someone, not just me or Tom...'

'Go on, Dad. I can take it.'

'Things like, "No, not Penelope and Philippa, I want them to be Poppy and Pippa,' but the scariest thing, just before she died, was, "You win, Estelle, now I'm finished", and then her whole voice changed when she said, "We can't all live again but my twins must have that chance".

I can feel all the heat draining from me and I want to find Pippa.

'Dad, are you thinking what I'm thinking?'

'I don't believe in ghosts but I do think Estelle took over Stella's body just before she died.'

'Estelle perhaps didn't live again but she wanted her twins to live again. Dad, I'm scared now. What if Estelle's twins are ghosts trying to take over Pippa's and my bodies? It all makes sense now. In a way, Stella WAS Estelle and Penelope and Philippa ARE me and Pippa. I *have* to go and find Pippa *now*.'

We all jump as the landline rings loudly.

'Poppy, I need you to come and see all this. Can you come now? *Please*. I'll meet you at the castle door.'

Dad says he'll walk with me and I can almost hear his heart beating as fast as mine as we go through the trees as dusk is falling and casting ominous shadows.

Pippa meets us on her own and leads us upstairs to a wide landing in the castle which has Wi-Fi. Her voice is shaky. 'There's a whole bunch of texts on my old phone and loads more on my laptop – images of you and me together. How did that happen?'

'I guess we know who now, but not how?' I say.

'You mean...'

'Our mother Stella's ghost; she calls herself Estelle. What's in the texts?'

'Well,' begins Pippa, 'they're from the same number 31101 600 613. I texted first: *'You said to text you, from Pippa.'*

'So Pippa, you've met our twin Poppy.'

'What do you mean OUR twin?'

This is now Philippa. She, Penelope and Estelle are sharing that phone.

'You're really Philippa, not Pippa. She's really Penelope not Poppy. Estelle gave us our names.'

'Who's Estelle?'

'She's our first mother who's looking after our future.'

'What do you mean OUR mother?'

'Don't you see? You are me and I am you or, Poppy is Penelope and Pippa is Philippa.'

'I'm not sure I do see but I'll take your word for it. What future is Estelle looking after for us?'

'First things first: to get to the future, you'll both have to explore the past.'

'How?'

'We'll have to hurry; there are only 13 days left to change the course of our history. Your first stop is the Ballindourie

kirkyard; you'll know what we're looking for when you get there.'

'*What's going to happen after 13 days?'*

'*Goodbye. No more for now – but check your email inbox.'*

'Oh, Pippa, that's scary. Dad and I were thinking Estelle had taken over our mum Stella's body and now it looks like these other twins are trying to steal our bodies. I never believed in that stuff but I think we have to now.'

'I'm afraid I agree, girls,' Dad says putting an arm around each of our shoulders. 'There are strange forces at work here but try not to be afraid.'

'Oh, Poppy ... and Dad... it's funny calling you that because Rory's my dad too ... it's like reincer... reancer...'

'Reincarnation,' I say, glad that Katie and I did that research on the internet in London.

'I don't know if that's good or bad,' Pippa says. 'Are you scared?'

'I should be, but do you know what? I'm not.'

'Me neither,'

'Come on, my two girls, we all need some sleep.'

'No I want to see the images on the laptop,' I insist.

Pippa clicks on a folder of pictures newly downloaded from an email address she tells me disappeared before she could check it. How weird is that?

'I didn't think to look straightaway at the email address. Well you don't, do you?' Pippa says. 'I wanted to reply but the message was deleted.'

OMG we're both there, me with my birthmark and Pippa without it but we're different. The hair's brown but it looks wavy and unbrushed and we're wearing something horrible – like brown sacking with muddy bits on it.

'I wouldn't be seen dead in that!' Pippa says and we laugh nervously because we're not sure if the twins in the picture are us or not, or if they are alive or dead, or whether we'll be

81

joining them in some sort of limbo between today and the past and the future. Totally unsettling it is. We seem to be walking hand in hand in different places, wild places, with trees and mountains and water, maybe Loch Ness.

'This could be around here,' Pippa says, 'but it all looks different from anything I've seen... except maybe that mountain,' she says pointing at the background of one of the pictures.'

'Time to go,' Dad says again, more firmly and I'm too tired to say no. We've got to visit Ballindourie kirkyard tomorrow.

Chapter 14:
Thirteen Days to Go

Pippa picks me up at 9 o'clock and we go straight to the kirkyard. Mum, Dad and Ralph are sleeping in, exhausted after the journey and Pippa's parents are busy working around the castle.

'I never look around the graves even though we're here every Sunday; it seems too spooky.'

'Huh,' I say, 'we might be spooks ourselves. What are we looking for?'

'I'm guessing some very old grave.'

'Ah, of course, 400 pix one for every year. That means like sixteen hundred and something.' We walk around until we find crumbling old headstones and try to find one that's clear enough to read; they all seem to be covered in green mould. We both know we're getting close when a shiver goes up both our spines and we cling to each other.

'Look!' Pippa shouts. I can just make out P E N   O P   and then D V N P ORT near the top but the rest is clear BORN **31** ocTOVER 1600 DIED 9 AUGUST 1613.

'Oh my giddy ghost, that's me and I died when I was…um… 13. Oh no, I'm, no *we're* 13 NOW.'

'Oh … and 9th of August is 13 days from today,' Pippa adds, 'And the other me said we had to hurry. I wonder when I died and if our mother was dead. We have to keep looking. Come on Poppy, quick.'

We scrabble around all over and just as we are about to give up, we see some more mounds and slabs on the other side of an ancient hedgerow and ditch.

'Let's try over there,' we both say. And we find it – a clear inscription reading: **EsTelle DaVenport b. 1581 d. 1626 ag'd 45 wife of SiMeon DaVenport mother of twins PeNelope (deceased) and PhiliPpa grandmother of JoSeph and ChaRles.**

'I wonder why she was buried outside the churchyard,' I ask and Pippa reckons she might have been disgraced.

'And you know what this means,' I say. 'You must have had two sons before Estelle died, so you lived much longer than I did.'

'Listen to us. We're talking as if we really believe we've lived before.'

'I think we should speak to Mr Forsyth. He might know something.'

'Who's he?'

'He's the minister o' the Ballindourie Kirk. He sometimes looks up stuff in a big book he keeps locked up at the back o' the Kirk.'

We find Reverend Forsyth sorting out hymn books inside the church and after he gets over the shock of seeing two Pippas, we take him to the two graves and explain that the twins must have been our ancestors. We'll stick to that for now.

'How can we find out more about them?' Pippa asks.

'Well now, Pippa, we can try the Old Parish Registers. These were supposed to have been kept from 1552 by law, but not many Kirks have complete records. Mind you, Ballindourie wasn't too bad, being near the castle where the gentry might have been nagging about keeping records of important folks. Shall we have a look? I'll need to put on my white, cotton gloves though and I have to ask you not to touch the big books; they're falling to bits, I'm afraid.'

He rushes off excitedly and we run after him until he collects a bunch of huge keys one of which opens a creaky old door into a fusty, musty room full of dust, leather bound books and some old silver cups and yellowed cloths that might once have been white. I scream as something sticks to my face.

'Och, lassie, it's jist a cobweb. I hardly ever get in here,' the gentle, white-haired old man says. 'I seem to remember an old story about a young herb wife and her mother looking after the lady at the castle when she was confined.'

'What's confined?' Pippa asks.

'*Just about to have a baby or just after it's born,*' my ghost says in my voice.

'I'm surprised a young lassie like you should know that old word.'

'Oh I read it somewhere,' I say quickly. Pippa winks.

'Right,' says the minister. 'What were the dates? Ah yes, 1580 – 1600; they started a bit late and the records don't seem to be complete but you never know. Well now, here we are under births: Estelle Lyndsay, born 21st November 1584, Mother Elizabeth Lyndsay née Bruce, Herbwife, Father James Lyndsay, Farmer.

'Her mother *was* a herbwife,' I gasp. 'I love my herb garden.'

'Ah weel, if she's yer ancestor, it's in yer blood,' the old man says innocently. It's a good thing he doesn't know what we know.

'I want to know more about the twins,' says Pippa impatiently.

'Let's see, October 1600 might be in this book. Nothing for September births – oh dear the book's beginning to tear. Ah, October ... yes...Here it is: Philippa Davenport b. 31st Oct 1600 to Mother Estelle Davenport, herbwife/ midwife née Lyndsay, Father Simeon Davenport, brewer and gardener, and look, there's another entry for Penelope Davenport (younger) and dittos all the way across. Now, fancy that. Just like you two. All these years, Pippa and I didn't know you had a twin.

You know you were baptised Philippa Drummond and I've known your mum and dad all their lives. I married them twenty years ago. Now fancy that.' He's shaking his head in disbelief.

I'm dying to say something but Pippa's got a finger on her lips. We both know what the next question is.

'Is there more about the twins?' we ask in perfect unison.

'Ah, let's see Deaths 1601 – 1650; that should cover it. What was the date on Penelope Davenport's grave?'

'1613.'

'Ah, here we are: died August 9th 1613 tragically drowned proving innocence of witchcraft following the death of Baron Robin Douglas at one day old. Now isn't that dreadful?'

'You mean they thought she was a witch and tried to drown her.'

'Yes. If a witch floated she was guilty but if she drowned she was innocent.'

'But that's not fair, she died innocent.' Pippa says.

'And worse, if she floated they burned her because they thought she was guilty.'

'But I, um, she was only a girl.` Is he giving me a puzzled look?

'Girls of thirteen were women and often mothers in those days,' Mr Forsyth explains.

'I want to know how long the other twin lived,' Pippa says raising her eyebrows and pointing at her chest, behind the minister's back. He's getting more and more interested but he's still turning the pages slowly with his white gloves in case the pages turn to dust. We find out that Philippa lived until 1649 when she died of 'fever caused by plague' and that she was survived by her husband, Robert and two sons, Joseph and Charles.

'49 was a good old age in those days and perhaps she'd have lived longer without the plague.'

'Oh we forgot Estelle. What did she die of? It was 1526?'

'Here we are. Oh, it's hard to read, it's so faded. Can you make it out? Your eyes might be better than mine.'

Pippa and I peer at the faint script. *Estelle Davenport d. O t 1 15 6 u ide fe le mind hearing vo es of vil ir ts.*

'Oh, never mind. We'll never be able to read it,' Pippa says quickly. 'Thanks Mr Forsyth, we really appreciate your time but we better get back before they think we've got lost.'

'Any time girls, I'm glad I was helpful. Interesting. Very interesting.'

Out of earshot, Pippa can't wait to speak. 'I know why she was buried outside the churchyard. I read suicide caused by feeble mind, hearing voices of evil spirits.'

'How could you read that?'

'I must have been at her funeral. She would have been my mother and I outlived her. Hang on, I didn't find out about my marriage.' We dash back to the church before the minister has locked everything away.

'Wait, Mr Forsyth. Can we find out about the marriage of Philippa and what she did? I'm sorry to bother ye again.'

'No trouble, Pippa. I'm fair intrigued myself. Wait, let's take a guess. We could start with 1616 when she was sixteen. This might take a while. No, nothing up to 1625. Maybe I'll try earlier. Oh, here we are: On June 20th 1615 at Ballindourie Kirk, Robert MacColla, age 19, bachelor, brewer and gardener, and Philippa Davenport, age 15, spinster, confectioner and embroiderer.

'Oh My God,' I say, '– oh sorry Mr Forsyth – Oh my, she was only 15. She'd be breaking the law today.'

'Aye, that she would. Now, if that's all ladies, I need my morning coffee and it's time you went home.'

'Well I wasnae a herb wife,' Pippa says on the way home. 'I bet I didnae want to go the way o' my deid twin.'

I'm thinking out loud, though I have a funny feeling my twin can read my thoughts. 'Can you see what's going on? Penelope and Estelle both died unnatural deaths.'

'Huh, the plague's nae a great way to die, either.'

'Estelle's soul's floating about trying to get her twins together.'

'And she's managed.'

'But there's something else troubling her.'

'Estelle outlived her daughter and it was a horrible death and this must hae driven her glaikit.'

'And Penelope's been stalking me since my 13th birthday. I told you about the ghost floating around my Halloween party. She must be a lost soul too and that's why I'm feeling her more than you're feeling Pippa.'

'I thought it was my crap internet connection.'

'Could be that too – but maybe you are the one who's there to help Estelle and Penelope get out of Limbo, back into the real world – or worse.'

'I think Estelle failed when Stella died,' Pippa continued.

'I'm scared Pippa. If Stella died, perhaps I could die.'

'Oh, dinnae say that Poppy, I've just found ye.'

'I wonder what we're supposed to hurry to do before 13 days' time,' I say.

'Wait a minty! Fit's the date and fit happened 13 days from now aw these years ago?

'July 28th + 13 – that's August 9th. Isn't that when... oh, I don't know, it's too scary to think about.'

We rush back to Heather Cottage to find the others just waking up and having breakfast. There's another family in the nearby Bracken Cottage and two brothers, Peter and Michael, around Ralph's age, have come knocking at the door. They're going to a terrific Adventure Park tomorrow, they say, and would we like to join their family on a visit? Perfect for Ralph and perhaps I can give the excuse that I'd like to spend some time with my new-found twin. We twins have decided we'd better keep our visit to the kirkyard and the minister quiet – though this probably won't last long in this place. Pippa says everybody knows everybody else's business in about five minutes around here.

Pippa goes home for lunch and we make a quick trip to the local big supermarket for supplies. We have the best ever fish and chips for lunch – not sure about the Scottish pickled egg. I wonder where Voice has gone, or Voices?

We're putting in some time looking for the monster when Peter and Michael come over with a football and Pippa comes with an invitation to look around the castle. (I know she means the Wi-Fi balcony). Mum and Dad need a rest, they say, and Ralph sets off to play around Bracken Cottage.

Nobody seems to have said anything about our trip to the Kirk yet so maybe the minister's a bit less of a gossip than we thought. We switch on our phones as soon as we get upstairs. Mine starts whistling so I set it on vibrate.

'Now you understand a bit of what happened but I need you to do something else. Go south along the loch side until you find a bumble bee willow tree hanging over a cliff.

'Why?' I text.

'You'll know why when you go under the tree. You need to go in the morning.'

'Why?'

'What happens then will take some time. Goodbye.'

'How much time?'

'Some time but, for you, no time at all.'

There's nothing on Pippa's phone and we both know goodbye means goodbye so she decides to get her laptop from her house behind the castle, leaving me to soak up the atmosphere. It feels like I've been here before but I don't recognise any of the heavy furniture or the huge paintings on the wall. But, there's something familiar about a heavily carved

89

chest on the landing at the top of the stairs. My main feelings are sadness and fear and, by the time Pippa gets back I'm shivering.

She boots up before she notices: 'What's the matter, Poppy? You look as if you've seen a ghost.'

'Not seen – but I'm feeling more than one – many more. I can almost hear them and smell them but I can't see them. And something terrible is going to happen or maybe it has already happened.'

'Let's see what's in the inbox. That's where the pix of both of us were so it must be Estelle on email. Maybe she didna hae a smartphone.' This makes us giggle, but next moment we're staring at a blurry picture of three people, a woman with long, tangled red hair and very pale skin, a man with black hair and broad shoulders and a girl with brown hair, probably one of the twins. We can't see the birthmark.'

'I bet that's our mother and father and one of us, but why is it so fuzzy and dark? Huh, must be because it's 400 years old.'

'Och, these auld cameras were useless,' says Pippa and our giggles are more hysterical this time. 'Oh phooey, I forgot to check the email address again and everything's deleted, even the picture. Oh no.'

My phone vibrates and a text comes through with the image so we reckon somebody back then or up in the air has a phone. And they definitely have some unfinished business that involves us. Who are we? Pippa and Poppy or Philippa and Penelope and who's the managing director of this project? And how is it possible for medieval people to have a handle on 21st century technology. Something really big must be happening in Limboland. Maybe they've gone forward through the centuries as well as back.

Pippa's telling me it must be dangerous to meddle like this with the supernatural and I'm agreeing but we're not being given much choice. We reckon Estelle is the driving force and she's a strong one and I'm trying to remember if I've ever seen a photograph of our mother Stella and the truth is I never have. Rosie Mum always said our dad found it too hard to look at her picture but I don't know if pictures of Stella still exist.

'Let's go to Heather Cottage and ask your dad what Stella looked like.'

'I think I'd rather ask Rosie. Don't say anything Pippa; I'll choose my moment.'

'Righty oh, Poppy.'

So we're Pippa and Poppy, now, like we've known each other all our lives as we wander along the woodland path with dappled sunlight dancing around us as it peeps through the trees.

'You smelt the tea, girls,' Rosie says as she takes the tartan tea cosy off the big teapot, both provided in the holiday cottage. 'There's some millionaire's shortbread, your favourite Poppy.'

'Mine too,' Pippa says. 'Pippa and Poppy two peas in a pod,' she adds and we laugh happily. I can see Mum and Dad giving each other another funny look, but it looks a happy one, full of relief. I think they think it's job done for the spooks. If only they knew.

Arrangements have been made for Peter and Michael's family and Mum, Dad and Ralph to have a long day out at the adventure park. Ralph is thrilled about canoeing and climbing and *loads* of other stuff he says. Pippa and I are invited of course but of course we say no and everyone understands, of course.

Dad is messing about outside with Ralph so we ask Rosie what Stella looked like and if there are any pictures hidden away.

'I was waiting for you to ask one day. There are pictures in a black magic chocolate box locked in the safe at home, but I can tell you she was very pretty with milky white skin and red hair which she kept in a shiny bob. She was a bit New Age in her ideas on alternative medicine and shooting stars bringing good luck around July and August. She always said shooting stars take lost souls to Heaven. You would have loved her. Your brown hair is halfway between your dad's black hair and her red hair; everybody said that at the time.

'Was her hair like Uncle Tom's?' I ask.

'A bit brighter than his and straighter.'

Pippa asks who Uncle Tom is so we have lots to talk about as we go for a stroll down to the water's edge. We decide to ring him on my smartphone, so now we have to clamber up to the top of the hill.

'Hello Poppy, I've been waiting for your call. Have you met your twin yet?'

'Yes. How did you know?'

'Voices again. No, I'm lying; your dad phoned. I'm sorry we lied about her being adopted; he thought it was for the best but then he was sorry and it was too late.'

'My twin is fantabulous, Uncle Tom, and we're Pippa and Poppy, two peas in a pod now. You can say hello in a minute but first, are you sure you haven't been hearing voices again because we have?'

'As it happens, I have.'

'Who's Estelle, Uncle Tom?'

'Ah, she's been talking to you, has she?'

'Uncle Tom, are you saying maybe the voices are real?'

'Let's see what happens.'

'We'll let you know when we find out more, but don't be scared. It's okay, I'm sure. Here's Pippa.'

'Hello Pippa. This is your uncle, your mum's brother. I hope we'll meet someday soon.'

'Hello … Uncle Tom. It's smashin' tae meet Poppy but we're still really confused about what's goin' on. How did we get put together like this?'

'No doubt you'll find out soon. Keep me posted.'

'Okay. I'd better go,' Pippa says and hands me the phone and I hit speaker.

'Bye, Uncle Tom. Ring if any more voices come; we might be needing them,' Pippa and I say in exact unison, leaving us wondering how that happened.

'Take care, girls. There are strange forces out there that nobody fully understands.'

'We will,' we say, once again, exactly together.

'Well, I can hear you've got it together. Bye.'

'Bye.'

And he's gone – leaving an odd feeling. I wonder where he was the day the holiday brochure landed on my bed. Is our uncle the link between 2013 and the Never- Never highway through limbo to the past?

Chapter 15:
Behind the Bumble Bee
Willow Tree

We two are heading south along the loch side, a picnic lunch in our backpacks, after I was allowed a sleepover at Pippa's home. We've got a whole long day to sort out whatever Estelle's ghost tells us will 'take some time'. I'm feeling mega excited and Pippa looks flushed and flustered too. After chatting for hours getting to know each other, we had a good night's sleep with no voices, texts or emails but, just as we round a bend, the footpath splits and Voice speaks.

'Take the low road near the water.'

'But naebody ever walks there; it's too dangerous. Can we nae tak the top road ower the cliff? There's a grand view there.'

'*Nae the day Philippa - and not today Penelope,*' Voice chirps with a chuckle. She's playing a game and she knows well that I'm from London and my twin is from the banks of Loch Ness. Maybe Estelle's spirit brought Pippa here in the first place – and then somehow got me here to join her. We do as we're told and scramble round the rocky cliff, into the water and out again and over some sharp broken stones. The ancient weeping willow, with its bumble bee, pussy willow catkins now faded and dropping in this late summer, is right there, just as I imagined it.

'I've never seen the lambs' tails so late,' my more knowledgeable twin says. 'My granny says this tree is a sign o' sorrow.

'What a beautiful old tree. It does look as if it's crying,' I say.

I suppose we'd better look ahint it.' We hold hands and look at each other, take a deep breath and step gently behind the droopy curtain of leafy branches, into a high cave, lit by the morning sun through narrow cracks in the sides and ceiling. The floor of the entrance to the cave is covered in sand, small pebbles and rotting leaves but there seems to be a clear path leading deep into the darkness towards goodness knows where. We set off along the path; walking is easy as the roof is high and there's still some light coming through the holes. It becomes darker and danker and strange new smells begin to fill the air. Familiar smells perhaps? We hang on to each other as we hear a pad, slap, pad slap and a crackling coming towards us and see a glow of light as a young boy carrying a burning torch turns a corner and beckons us to follow him. My feet feel heavy and uncomfortable and I find I'm carrying a small bunch of something fragrant, perhaps lavender, but I can barely see through the smoke. The lavender smell is welcome as there are so many other nasty smells around.

95

'It smells like somebody's forgotten to flush the lavvy,' Pippa says. 'Hoi, I've found a lavender posy in my hand. Where the spooks did that come from?'

'Maybe lavvies haven't been invented,' I say catching on to the local dialect and coming to terms with a really crazy and alarming idea. We've landed back in The Middle Ages!

'Who are you?' I shout at the boy we're following. He covers his mouth with his fingers and carries on walking along the winding path.

'He's dumb,' Pippa says. 'I know him. He was Dugal, a gardener at the castle in our first life. It's comin' back tae me. I used to make the puddings for the Laird and his Lady and their guests when they had their banquets at the castle.'

It's getting brighter as the tunnel is now being lit by torches on the wall. I get a shock as I look down at what I'm wearing and across at what my twin is wearing. Where was the switch to the wooden and leather shoes, the baggy brown dresses with sleeves tied on with leather laces and the white aprons tied behind our necks and at the back of our waists?

'What the fuzzy fairy do we look like, Sis?' I'm getting used to my twin's jokey talk.

'Normal I hope. Can you imagine if we'd turned up in 1613 in trainers and denim shorts? We might have been burned at the stake or boiled in oil.'

'Do ye really think we're back there? Oh Poppy; what's gonna happen?'

We've started going uphill now and we're arriving at a set of steps, built of flattened earth, worn down into a dip in the middle and shiny, I imagine because so many people keep walking up and down them.

'We'll soon find out, Pippa.'

A woman in a dark green dress with some wooden thing across her shoulders, from which two huge wooden buckets are dangled, is heading into the tunnel we have just come out of.

96

'Where are you going? I ask. When she looks puzzled Pippa tries, 'Faur ye gaen?'

'Doon fur watter.'

'Tae the loch?'

'Aye, the work o'gan fur watter niver staps.'

We're being attacked by sounds, smells and noises as we follow the boy Dugal along a road made of the same flattened earth but with ruts and potholes filled with boulders and sprinkled with sand. The pad slap we'd heard was Dugal's broken shoes that he is struggling to keep on his feet, and now there is the thuddity thud of a horse's feet pulling a cart that creaks and clanks. The horse shakes his head and his tackle rattles and slaps before he purses his lips and makes that noise that only horses can make and there's no word for; it's something between a snort and a splutter, maybe.

'I call that a long mouth fart,' my clever twin says. She was definitely born first. I ask her how many different smells she can smell and between us we make a list: burning wood, horse manure, the lavvy, some kind of unfamiliar meat cooking, rotting vegetables, newly cut grass, body odour, some strange drink like beer or cider and a lovely smell of newly baked something, maybe bread.

'Don't tell me about 21st century pollution, ever again,' Pippa says taking the words out of my mouth.

People seem to be wandering around busily, women carrying pots on their heads or men clutching big curved knives under their arms, (scythes, Pippa says, for cutting the corn). The children are playing with cats or dogs or carrying baskets of apples or eggs and there seem to be pigs, cows and sheep all around and nobody thinks they've got 'oota the park' as Pippa says, which means 'out of their field' she tells me. Just as we're wondering why we're here (we've given up worrying about how) a pretty woman with long red hair and very green eyes crosses our path, forcing us to stop.

97

Chapter 16:
Can the Laird's Bairn be saved?

'Ye're here. None kens ye've been gone except me so stay quiet and go about yer usual tasks like I tell ye to.' It's definitely that second voice. Philippa's was the first, or was it Penelope's? We must look petrified as her next words are. 'Now Philippa and Penelope, that's who you are. Davenport is your family name after your father, Simeon Davenport, my husband, so it's aw legitimate. Dinna be afeared. I'm yer mither and I niver looed onybody mair.'

'Why did you bring us here?' I ask.

'We need to save the Laird's bairn and his lady. Did ye ken ye were a herbwife and midwife, Penelope?'

'I thought I might be.'

'Perchance this time the wee baron will live and his mother won't die of grief and you won't be drowned an innocent.' After our visit to the minister, we don't have to ask for any explanations. 'I see you understand they accused you of being a witch. It was Baron Gavin Douglas's grief that did it, turned all the people against ye.'

'How do you know I'll save the baby this time?'

'I don't. I've tried every century, bringing you into the world on Halloween in 1700, 1800, and 1900 but the bairn still died.'

'How did the baby die?'

'It was a yellow infection and fever that started 13 days before the birth and it got worse until the woman didna have any strength left to bring the poor mite into the world. He was pulled from her but his chest was so full of disease he only lived for one day; then the mother wept for two days and died herself. His lairdship blamed you.'

'Why me?'

He said you'd given her the poison ergot which killed them both but it's what you and I always used to stop the bleeding when a bairn was born.'

'Where were you?'

'A two day walk up the valley with another mother. She lived but Lady Isabella died. I've never forgiven myself for not being there for ye.

'Where was I?' Pippa asks.

'You were doon in the kitchens preparing the feast to celebrate the birth, and stitching the Christening gown in your spare time. Penelope, can you find the magic herbs to save this mother and child? I have turned time back three times now. We must not fail this time. My soul needs to rest.'

The desperate pain showing on our mother's face is tearing me apart and I can feel it tearing Pippa to bits too. This tortured woman has been wandering around with no rest for more than 400 years now.

'Antibiotics!' Pippa and I shout at exactly the same moment.

'We can do it. I'm almost sure. How long have we got?'

'Not long; Lady Isabella is weak and sick already and is refusing to eat.'

'We have to go back to our world for the medicine,' I say.

'Then go! And please, please, hurry.'

We set off into the tunnel escorted by Dugal again. He always seems to be next to us, watching and waiting for who knows what. He won't go as fast as we'd like him to so we chat along the way.

'Have you noticed Estelle changes her words when she speaks to me from when she speaks to you?'

'Aye, I mean yes; most Scots can do that.'

'But could they do that in The Middle Ages?'

'She's not there; she's wandering through purgatory looking for a place to rest. The minister talks about lost souls in The Kirk sometimes.'

I'm glad somebody thinks there might be some sense in this whole confusing business but my mind keeps coming back to the real world, *my* real world.

'Pippa, can you remember when penicillin was invented? If it was before 1900, then we could be wrong about Lady Isabella's illness. Estelle tried 1900 and it failed.'

'I'm trying to remember; I think it was eighteen something but we have to try.'

'What'll happen if we fail?'

'You'll die again Poppy.'

'Does that mean I'll die in 2013 too?'

'I hope not. Come on let's overtake Dugal. We have to hurry and find Sandy McPherson.'

'Who's he?'

'The chemist and we'll need to see the doctor.'

'Why?' (We can't take him with us. What is she thinking?)

'For a prescription silly.'

We're puffing and panting in our hurry and choking on the smoke from Dugal's torch but the daylight finally starts coming through the cracks and he turns back. Look at the state of us, dressed in medieval clothes and reeking of smoke and olden days. Estelle's forgotten these details in her clever, time-travelling supernatural plan. But she hasn't. There on the shelf are our backpacks with our clothes neatly folded on top and our trainers next to them. We strip off our dresses and many petticoats and our shoes of wood and fur to find we're still wearing our bras and pants. Unbelievable! We find our socks in our trainers and throw them on and our T shirts and denim shorts, and run.

'What's the time Poppy?' As I'm walking I dive into the side pocket of my backpack to find my phone.

'I don't believe this. It's 09:30.'

'That means we were only in 1613 for...'

'No time at all,' we say together.

How can that be? We contemplate the possibility that time has stood still before looking at the phone to find that time's moving on again.

'Oh no we have to get a move on!' we shout in one voice. How weird.

We rush to the doctor's surgery but he's off on his rounds so my bold twin gets me chatting to the receptionist, who can't believe how alike we are. I'm asking her to look closely to find a difference which is just enough time for Pippa to rip off the top of the prescription pad on her desk and stuff it down her T shirt.

'It's life and death, Poppy and a very good cause,' she says and I get over being shocked as she flattens out the paper. 'We've got five blank sheets here and I know I can copy his signature; it's just a stupid squiggle but we need to know what antibiotics to write.'

'I can Google on my smartphone.'

'Up the brae, quick.'

There are so many different things for treating mothers and babies for so many problems like Group B Streptococcus, chorioamnionitis, endometritis and oh it's too much to take in. It looks like clindamycin, gentamicin and ampicillin might cover them all. Pippa reckons she can copy Molly, the medical secretary's roundy handwriting but then she changes her mind and uses block capitals. She doesn't know how many to put but I remember Rosie getting 7 days of 500mg 3 times a day for her chest infection so I tell her to put 21x500gm for all three and squiggle the doctor's signature. We carefully fold the two spare prescriptions and put them in the pocket of my backpack

101

next to my phone, in case they might be needed. We rush to the chemist and tell him there's a mother nearly nine months gone with a terrible infection and a fever burning her up.

'Where's this woman? Have you got a prescription?'

'Here,' says Pippa, and by way of distraction in case he looks too closely she rattles on quickly. 'She's a gypsy woman, way out in the sticks and the doctor's in an agitated state. Please hurry, Mr McPherson, the baby might die.'

'Och Pippa Drummond, you're making an old man rush too much. Give me a minute; I'll be as fast as I can.' He rushes off to the back of the shop and comes back with three boxes and puts them in a paper bag. 'You're lucky I had them in stock. There's no payment for a pregnant woman, but tell the doctor I'll be chasing him up for her details and make sure she has three doses today before she goes to bed. She should be okay in a day or two. Is this your cousin, Pippa?'

'She's my twin. '

'I never knew you had a twin.'

'Neither did I. Oh, by the way, when was penicillin invented?'

'It was 1928 before it was perfected.'

'Thanks. Later. Got to rush.'

I would love to have waited to see the look on his face but there is no time to waste and we're soon at the cave. This time we dress by ourselves for 1613 and leave our 2013 gear on the rock. I check my phone for the time and it's exactly 12:00 midday. There aren't any pockets in any of the many petticoats or the dress or even the apron so I pick up a petticoat and try to fold the medicine into a corner. The boxes are too bulky so I take the strips out; thank goodness it's written on them what the pills are. Now it's easy to tie them safely into a corner with a double knot. Dugal is waiting and he knows we have to rush so we pad, slap crackle at double speed all the way through to where Estelle is waiting anxiously at the top of the worn steps.

102

'Hurry Penelope, Lady Isabella's already breaking into a fever.'

'We walk quickly into the castle, yes, it's the same Ballindourie Castle, and upstairs to the bedchamber where her ladyship is on a huge four poster bed behind thick, blue curtains.

'Look Poppy, there's the exact same chest that's in the castle today.'

I'm too busy trying to imagine what a 21st century midwife might do. Thank goodness for *Holby City*, *Call the Midwife* and *There's One Born Every Minute* on TV. I do believe I'll know what to do when the baby comes, that is if the mother is well enough to go into labour. I don't even notice that Philippa, has been whisked away to another part of the castle and Estelle has gone too.

'Bring me clean drinking water and hot water to wash her ladyship and plenty of clean cloths.'

The two maids are looking puzzled.

'I'm sorry ma'am; the water's nae guid for drinking. She can have the honey mead in the jug by her bed. We'll try and get some water on the fire to heat but it'll be a while.'

'Thank you, that's fine. See if you can find some fruit and anything else tasty to eat. Her ladyship will need to build up her strength.'

I fill a stone cup with mead and make the weak Lady Isabella drink it all with an ampicillin pill, the strongest antibiotic of the three. 'Don't worry your ladyship; this medicine will work, but you need to drink lots of liquid and try to eat something.'

A maid rushes in with a slice of pie with a strong smell and some blackberries, apples and plums.

'It's a pigeon pie, ma'am and there's a chicken and vegetables boiling on the water heating fire; we got the woodcutters to bring mair wood.'

103

'Thank you. That's excellent. Is there anything more for her to drink?' Is this girl calling *me* ma'am? I can't be much older than *she* is.

'I'll keep some fresh milk after the milking and look out some apple perry. I hope her ladyship feels better soon,' she says before curtseying and leaving the room.

I have a lot to learn about seventeenth century life I can see. I'm out on the balcony overlooking the countryside leading down to the loch in the distance. It's a waiting game now. More sounds, unfamiliar to the 21st century world, are reaching me: chickens squawking and scratching, the chop, chop, chopping of wood, the neighing of horses, the bleating of sheep, the lowing of cows and a loud call of what I can see are peacocks wandering near the castle. I wonder if they eat them like chickens. I have washed her ladyship's face, hands and body and removed some grubby bedclothes and replaced them with clean ones from that wooden chest which is still there in 2013. She has eaten a little pigeon pie and two plums and finished all the honey mead in the jar. She has slept a little and the sun is over its highest point in the late summer sky. I hear her stirring so I go back in to give her another antibiotic with hot milk and bread with honey that a maid has just brought. When the sun goes down, she can have the 3rd pill for the day and I hope that starts to cure her.

I haven't seen my medieval mother or my medieval twin all day and when my patient has her 3rd pill with apple perry and some chicken and vegetable dinner and falls into a deep, healing sleep, I'm hoping I can leave her with a maid and go and find them.

As I'm leaving the room, a deep and anxious voice asks, 'How is she, Penelope?'

'Better I think, Your Lordship.'

'Your Lordship? You usually call me Baron Gavin.'

'Sorry, I'm a bit tired making sure she eats and drinks and has her medicine.'

'Her herbs, you mean?'

'Yes… Baron.' He seems to know me well but I only have the faintest memories of him and everyone else in 1613, even my mother. I suppose that's understandable after 400 years.

'You can go now. I'll send for you if you are needed. Thank you. My wife means the world to me.'

'Have you seen my sister Philippa?'

'She's in the kitchen painting the marchpane. I've just been there to arrange for my dinner to be served. We've just got back from the boar hunt.'

'Thank you … Baron Gavin.'

I have no idea where to find the kitchen or what a marchpane is but I follow my nose downstairs and find Pippa, now Philippa, decorating a cake with gold paint and a feather.

'Oh Poppy…Penelope, I've been grinding sugar and almonds for hours. Look I've got blisters. The chief cook wants a second cake for the celebration so I've spent all afternoon making marzipan and squeezing it into the same shape as this one I have to paint with gold. And they call it marchpane not marzipan.'

'I know, the baron told me you were painting the marchpane; I didn't know what he meant.'

'You met him? Everybody down here is terrified of him. He's got some temper I hear.'

'Well he was fine to me, maybe a bit distant, but he seemed worried about his wife. He seems to love her a lot.'

'Penelope, I am exhausted. If I don't rest, I think I'll die.'

'Philippa, we know you're not going to die for a long time. You marry and have two children and become a confectioner. Guess what; some little maid called me ma'am?'

'Me too; we seem to be quite important around here.'

105

'We have to stay,' I say. 'I can't trust anyone else to give Lady Isabella her pills. And somebody might give her herbs that could harm her.'

Philippa nods and I check that the pills are still safely knotted in my petticoat. I wonder when pockets were invented. Just then, Estelle comes in anxious for news. I tell her Lady Isabella has taken the medicine, is eating well, has slept and has cooled down.

'That's good. That didn't happen the last three times.'

'The correct medicine hadn't been invented by then. It'll take seven days but I think this time she will be cured.'

'I hope so. Now come to eat and sleep; the day is over. There's some chicken and a plum pie and yer auld bed is ready.'

Our mother keeps her distance but we follow her to a cottage behind the castle which must have been where we grew up, if only I could remember. Philippa reckons it's not far from her 2013 cottage or it might even be on the same site. The food is tasty enough though not much like anything we've tasted before and we wash it down with beer.

'Where's our father?' Philippa asks just as I was about to.

'He'll be late home tonight; they took the old horse and wagon up to the moor to collect heather for more ale. Most of the castle stocks will be needed for the celebrations. Go to sleep. You'll see him tomorrow; he will not notice you haven't been here for 400 years.'

We settle down on the low wooden bed with its straw mattress which isn't that uncomfortable though it would be nice to have a pillow. I peep under the mattress and find it is crisscrossed rope that's holding it up. There are no sheets but although we are sharing a double bed, we have a woollen blanket and a sheepskin rug each. I try using the sheepskin as a pillow but it's too rough so I wrap it in one of my three

106

petticoats. Poor Pippa has conked out without a pillow; it must be hard work being a medieval kitchen maid.

Next morning Estelle wakes me with a shake. I must have slept through. 'Come on pit on this ploden cloak; there's a maid waiting for ye and it's a cauld mornin',' my mother says, wrapping me in a checked blanket.

'Come ma'am. I saw ye tied yer herbs in yer kirtle. She needs ye.'

Fear grips me when I think of what might happen so we run. Lady Isabella is pouring with sweat and she thinks the baby is coming early. I have no idea but I wing it. 'You're fine, Lady Isabella. They're probably false labour pains. Just stay calm and you must take your next pill.'

'Pill?'

'The new medicine.'

She washes down the pill with milk and luckily the pains stop and she wants porridge and honey mead, which is a good sign. Then she falls asleep again. I'm thinking 2013 nursing would want her to get up and move around a bit so I'll encourage her to get out of bed when she wakes up. I don't have to. She joins me on the balcony where I've come to get some fresh air and sun, now that it has appeared. Medieval buildings are musty and smelly but I suppose everyone is used to it.

'Good Morning, Penelope. I do believe I feel much better. I'm as big and heavy as a horse but I feel good. I really do.'

'That's wonderful,' I say with a smile. She will never know how relieved I am. 'You have a bit of hard work to do soon but it will be a joy to have your new baby with you.'

'I can't wait to get this out of me, boy or girl, I don't care.'

'Like every mother before you and after you,' I say feeling her forehead. 'Your fever has gone now but you will have to take the pills for five more days before you are fully cured.' (I'm beginning to sound like a real midwife – but of course, in medieval times I *am*.) In 2013, my mother would be doing my washing and I'd be watching TV and listening to my music. How times have changed! I panic as I realise I may never get back there if things go wrong here.

'I think it would be good for you to walk about a bit to make you stronger. Can you do that your ladyship?'

She can, and we walk up and down and up and down the balcony, while she tells of her plans for the baby. If it's a boy, she'll call it Robin and a girl will be Mary after the poor dead Mary, Queen of Scots. There will be 200 guests for a feast at the castle and the Christening gown will be made of silk and 100 pearls will be stitched into it. Never has a baby been so eagerly awaited. The tragedy in 1613 must have been huge. Is it going to happen again?

The days go by and Lady Isabella is completing her course of antibiotics; her appetite is better and the baby has dropped down ready to be born. My mother has sent another young herbwife up the valley to the other mother and she is hovering in the background in case she is needed.

Mother and I go on a midwives' round to visit Aunt Sara, Estelle's sister, who has a boy and a girl and will soon have another. The toddlers, both in dresses, are beautiful but smelly and I'm wondering what people use for nappies. They don't in summer is the answer I discover, when Sara tells me to put ashes on the little boy's poo in the garden. I see why little boys wear dresses now.

Next we visit Aunt Cecily and her four month old baby boy. She tells me he will be a brave and strong May Day boy. He's ginger but Cecily has beautiful blue-black hair and bright blue eyes. This baby does have cloths that pass for nappies but I wouldn't like to have to wash them. Estelle tells me more when we leave:

'Cecily's boy had a twin but the wee lass died; she had the family mark.'

'What do you mean?'

'The butterfly on your cheek.'

'What?' I gasp. She's giving me a strange look so I say, 'Oh yes, I see,' but I don't and I'm scared. Will I die too, again? Is the butterfly a curse?

Philippa moans every night about the gross jobs she's being given like skinning a swan when it's still warm, piling the fire up for bread making or stacking wood in a different shape for water boiling. She complains that her face is burning, her hands are blistered and her fingers are so stiff she can't stitch the pearl buttons on to the Christening gown. I'm still terrified that something will go wrong with this birth and we'll never see modern times again. Our families must be worried and they'll have sent out a search party by now. What if anyone nicks our clothes from the cave? You never know, some druggies might find the cave when they're looking for a place to drug or whatever they do. This is all too stressful.

On the third evening we meet our dad, a big man with black hair and a black beard but he hardly pays us any attention. We ask our mother if he's always like this. 'Aye,' she says, 'when he's busy working, but he's better when there's free time.'

Lady Isabella is screaming her head off and my mother, thank goodness, and I head for the bedchamber. I've lost count of the date, although it hardly matters, except we *are* trying to rewrite history. This woman is not weak now and she's walking about and squatting and yelling and calling her husband the worst things you can imagine.

'My lady, I'm shocked,' my mother says laughing. She's heard it all before and she thinks it's a healthy sign. She tells me she's never seen Lady Isabella look so healthy. Is she crazy? The woman's about to give birth!

'She's usually so pale and skinny but now she looks healthy and well fed. It must be your doing Penelope and your herbs,' my mother tells me.

It's not long before her waters break and Lady Isabel starts the real hard work. The baby's head comes first and, one more push. and he's out and straightaway, he's yelling his head off. My mother has allowed me to be the one to deliver him.

'It's a boy! A lovely, big strong boy. Well done, your ladyship.' I'm shaking with joy and relief but still scared that something could go wrong. My mother takes care of the afterbirth and comes to me smiling to report there is no tearing and very little bleeding. Everything is fine and I've never seen a more beautiful smile than the one on my medieval mother's face.

The next second, there's a panic. Lady Isabella is worried. Is she bleeding from her breast? No, she just needs to nurse her new son who has been washed, swaddled and handed to her.

'I don't want a wet nurse,' she says. 'I want to feed him myself, at least for a little while. Hello Baron Robin Douglas,' she says to her son.

I didn't think I would feel sorry for all these medieval ladies who were made to hand over their babies to wet nurses. How sad that must have been, but today, in August 1613, we have changed history and made a few people very happy, including Pippa and me. OMG what happens now?

Chapter 17:
Will she let us go?

'I don't want you to go,' our medieval mother is saying and Pippa and I are panicking because she sounds as if she means it. What are we going to do? Could she keep us here until we live our seventeenth century life out? Well, yes she could, because we need Dugal to let us out through the tunnel and he's nowhere around.

'Stay for the feast.'

'But my family have to go home to London on August 9th and I don't know what the date is,' I say. 'And I was supposed to have died on that day in 2013.'

'It's August 5th,' Philippa says. 'You came on July 26th and 3 days later on the 29th we got the antibiotics and the baby was born the day after the course was finished which was 7 days later, August 4th and that's today, the 5th.'

'Can't you make that any more complicated?' I ask my twin.

'Then you can stay,' Estelle says. 'The feast is on the 3rd day after the birth, if mother and baby are well. But while you are here, time is not important.'

'That'll make it August 8th,' Pippa says, almost as if she doesn't mind staying. 'After all the hard work in the kitchen, I wouldn't mind tasting some of the stuff.'

'But both our families must be worried,' I say.

'Or perhaps no time has passed at all since we came through the tunnel. Don't you remember, Poppy?'

'I do but I don't believe we can have stayed a whole week here and no time has passed there. That's impossible.'

'Anything's possible in time travel,' Estelle says, 'Come on Penelope. You can visit the new baby and get lots of praise for making her ladyship well.'

'I suppose maybe we could stay, especially if time really has been suspended while we're here. But we have to leave on the 8th just in case it hasn't. You must promise.'

'I'll tell Dugal to get ready to take you through the tunnel while the feast is still going on,' Estelle says.

'What will happen to you now mother? Will you carry on living here and now?' I ask.

'Yes, I can, until I choose when I want to jump on a shooting star.'

'To Heaven,' we say as one.

She smiles.

'How will you explain our disappearance when we leave?' asks Pippa.

'You still have a double existence, Philippa and Penelope.'

'Does that mean we have two bodies, one in each time and place?' I ask.

'Yes, but I need someone to help me with your journey back. I can't do that myself. It needs someone else who still has a double existence.'

'Who can do that?' I ask.

'I know someone but he's far away in the forest until the day before the feast.'

It sounds like this feast is at the centre of everything.

Our father Simeon comes home early at last and he's finally smiling. The big brew of ale is complete and all's ready for the big day.

'How are my two bonny lassies the nicht? Tell me what you've been doing while your faither has been brewin' enough ale to float a dozen boats and quench the thirst o' abody frae fifty miles aroon.'

112

Pippa does the talking as her Scottish lilt can pass for medieval. She tells him about how I was the one who delivered the new baby and about the preparations for the feast and he listens happily before he nods off on his chair by the fireside.

'He's exhausted,' I say.

'Or maybe he's been tasting his work,' our mother adds.

The next two days rush past. I visit the new mother and baby often and they're doing fine much to Baron Gavin's delight. He is so thankful for my medicine for his wife and baby that he presents me with a beautiful gold pendant set with garnets and pearls, which I tell him I will always treasure. Secretly, I'm wondering if it will cross over into 2013. 400 years ago he would have been drowning me along with his sorrows and breaking my mother's heart.

I visit Pippa in the kitchen where amazing things are going on. The food list includes 1 boar, 2 deer, 100 pigeons, 50 chickens, 30 salmon, 3 barrels oysters, 3 swans and 2 peacocks which are going to have unspeakable things done to them. The swans and peacocks will be skinned, stuffed and brought to the table looking alive. Savoury pies, fruit pies, roasted vegetables, fresh bread and home-made cheeses are added to the menu. I watch pigs' trotters being boiled for a whole day to make gelatin for the desserts and help Pippa with the tricky job of painting yet another marchpane with a feather.

'How can people eat all this?' I ask the head cook whose name I have discovered is Agnes. She tells me she is English and has been employed to bring new ideas from the outside world to this remote castle in Scotland.

'They don't, but it is important that the guests have a choice.'

'What happens to the rest?'

'At these times, food and drink are shared with everybody. Nothing is wasted and nobody goes hungry. The fifty castle servants can eat for days and it's our duty to make sure

113

everyone in the district, especially the poorest, gets a hearty meal. But you know all this. Why are you asking?'

'Oh, because it seems so OTT.'

'You young lassies and your fancy new language. What's that?'

'Oh, it just means too much.' I keep forgetting that nobody knows that Pippa and I have crossed over. I'll have to be more careful.

Pippa and I are sharing our worries as we chat before we sleep. Why is it that we don't remember most of our medieval life but that some memories have come back? What if there's no time suspension and our parents think we disappeared ten days ago? What if they call the police and a search party find our clothes and backpacks in the cave? What if they find the phone and all these spooky messages? They might find the spare blank prescriptions we nicked from the doctor's surgery. What the spooks will the minister, the doctor and the chemist be telling everyone? And will they throw us in the nearest loony bin when we get back, *if* we ever get there?

I'm called to the bedchamber of Lady Isabella and baby Robin. She wants me to put in her ringlets before she sleeps.

'You do it so well Penelope,' she says, 'and I want to look my best.'

'I'll do my best, Your Ladyship' I say feeling glad of the recent practice on Katie. Did strange powers organise that?

We have to get up before sunrise tomorrow as there's a lot to do for the big day. Mother and baby will be spared any stress and I have to go and help to swaddle baby, first in thick cloths as nappies, a muslin shawl and then a new woollen shawl, while the lady's maids work on Lady Isabella's hair and jewellery and dress her in her prettiest embroidered surcote over a loose nursing gown. The idea is that young Robin should feed until he sleeps before he meets the people of his new world. There seems to be so much to think about. I have to

114

pinch myself to make sure I'm still alive, and that Lady Isabella and baby Robin are not dead this time and I'm not being tortured and about to be drowned. At times I think I have vague memories of that previous existence and it chills me to the bone. Could it all return to that and is this all a huge hoax, an inconceivable dream?

I take a moment to go and see Pippa who is rushing backwards and forwards to the banqueting hall with more and more platters of food to load on the already groaning five tables, 3 with swan centerpieces and 2 with peacock centerpieces. I have never before and will never again see such a spectacle, in the non-digital world. Pippa is excited. The woodcutters have come home and she's seen this fit guy called Robert. 'Poppy, he's gorgeous. I think he must be the Robert I'm going to marry. Are you *sure* Estelle is right that we have a double existence? Otherwise I'm not going *anywhere*.'

'Well, you're going to live and marry and have kids here before you die but I'm supposed to drown the day after tomorrow. I *have* to get home before then.'

'I didn't think of that. Sorry Sis, I don't want you to die,' she says, hugging me tight.

At last the banquet is underway for all the guests and Estelle calls us to our home before the servants' meal is served in the kitchens. 'I want you to meet someone who's going to help you cross back to your century. You might know him, Penelope.'

She turns her head towards a curtained sleeping area in a corner.

'You can come out now. Meet my brother Tam, head woodcutter for the castle.' A tall man with bushy red hair and a scruffy beard, dressed in leather and fur straightens himself up and smiles.

'Hi Poppy.'

'Uncle Tom!'

115

'Pippa, you talked to him on the phone. Uncle Tom this is Pippa.'

'Well I know her as Philippa and you as Penelope around here but you won't remember that. When I beam you back to 2013, your medieval personae will get back all the memories but Philippa and Penelope of 1613 will remember nothing about your visit because it hasn't happened yet. But I can get you home with full recollection of what has happened to you here, at least until it fades, like mine did.'

'Can you really do that and do we really have a double existence?' I ask.

'Indeed you have and so have I. There aren't many of us crossovers so you can count yourselves privileged. I'm going to travel with you through the tunnel, by the way, but before that we're going to enjoy the servants' banquet.'

Off we all go and my head is as full of burning questions as I'm sure Philippa's is. But they can wait.

It isn't long before the ale cheers us up and the food fills our stomachs and as I look across at my twin seated on the long bench on the other side of the long wooden table, I know she's thinking that perhaps life isn't so bad here in medieval times. When we go back to 2013, we'll leave it behind but our medieval personae will carry on this medieval life. Philippa will marry her Robert, and now I won't drown so I have no idea what will happen to me, except that I have a chance to live again. This whole idea is blowing my mind. Will we really remember all this when we leave? Did it actually happen?

At last, Uncle Tom nods his head towards the door so Estelle, Philippa and I follow him outside where Dugal is waiting with his torch.

'Mother,' I say, 'before we leave, can you tell me one thing? Did you come into our other mother Stella's body before she died?'

116

'I was always there. I am Stella and she is me. For me it is the end and I'm happy with that. I don't have a body to inhabit since Stella died so now we can both lay our heads down, content knowing that you, Penelope, have been saved from an unfair and untimely death to live your life alongside Philippa. Tam, please watch over my girls in the new world.'

'I promise, Estelle and good bye. Ah, look, the wild geese are forming their V ready to fly south to warmer climes. It's time for us to leave.'

As we gaze up into the sky, a breeze starts up and it seems to almost lift us off the muddy track away from the sounds, smells and tastes of 1613.

'Right Pippa and Poppy,' Uncle Tom says, 'two peas in a pod, are you ready for the journey back to the new world? Dugal, lead the way with your magic torch.'

'Where will you go, Mother?' I ask, blinking back tears.

'She has already gone,' says Uncle Tom.

'But she was just here…'

'Was she? Can you remember if she ever, ever, even once, touched you?'

'Uh … did she? I'm not sure.'

Chapter 18:
Unexplained

Of course, it all makes sense. Uncle Tom, the computer genius controlling everything through cyberspace in one world is as absolutely necessary as Uncle Tam, the head woodcutter providing heat and light in the other world.

'Why didn't you tell us what you were doing Uncle Tom?'

'At first my memories hadn't all come back and also it's a dangerous business crossing over. We haven't finished yet so come on; we have to get back through the tunnel immediately.'

'What's the hurry?'

'Estelle may already have vapourised so she might have lost her power to suspend time and give us protection. Dugal, please hurry.'

We overtake and pull him rather than push him so he has to slap pad at a run; I hope his feet aren't killing him. The light through the cracks is beginning to filter through and Dugal stops and waves goodbye.

'Thank you Dugal,' Tam shouts.

'Oh no, our bags have gone. There's been a search party and they've found them. That means we've lost the ten days!'

We turn back to Tam as he begins to speak. 'I think we're just in time. Come and see this.' He leads us back into the cave and there, where we had run so fast, four times now, is a solid rock face. 'That's totally impenetrable now,' he adds. 'None of us will get back there for now.'

'Look Uncle Tom, our gear has gone.'

'Hang on. I didn't trust that spot in case we lost the time delay and the police found them. I put them behind a rock over here. Ah yes here they are.'

Before we do anything, I dive into the pocket where I hope my phone still has some charge left. We all smile as it lights up and the time reads 12:00 midday.'

'That's the time we left,' Pippa says, 'but what's the date?'

'July 29th 2013. Yes!' I yell and Pippa and I jump around hugging each other.

'Where's Uncle Tom?'

He's nowhere to be seen.

'Do you think he's vapourised too?' Pippa asks.

'Were they both…?

'Ghosts,' we both gasp in one voice.

We change sadly out of our heavy medieval gowns and into our shorts and T-shirts, telling each other how good it is to feel comfortable and what bliss it is to get soft socks and comfy trainers on our tired feet.

'All we have to worry about is explaining away the prescription theft,' Pippa says.

'I'm really going to miss Uncle Tom, though; he was like my guardian angel in London. Come on let's get back to the cottage. We'll probably get there before they get home from their day out.'

'Och, I had so many questions I wanted to ask that new uncle of mine.'

There's no rush now so we wander back along the loch side, enjoying the view and chatting about all the things about the 21st century that we missed: sheets and pillowcases on a soft bed, ice cream, TV, smartphones, *pockets*, and a hundred other things.

'Hey, we haven't had our picnic,' I say.

'Fit's ma mither pit in here? It must be rotten after aw this time.' But it's not, so we sit down near the water and tuck into peanut butter and brown bread sandwiches, Irn Bru, crisps and an apple.'

'Missed the crisps too,' I mumble between mouthfuls.

119

We set off slowly towards Heather Cottage again asking each other if we'd miss anything from 1613.

'I wonder where Estelle and Tam went. I was just about to ask ...'

'Hey, you two, you can't get rid of me that easily.' Marching behind is Uncle Tom, minus the beard but in need of a haircut and dressed in baggy cords and a checked shirt like any normal 2013 sad uncle.

'I had to have a dip to get rid of the stench. Phoof, you two had better get into the shower before the others get home. That's the thing I hate about the old days; bath time only comes round every few years.'

'Oh yea, we do stink a bit,' says Pippa.

'Uncle Tom, where did that kooky phone number come from?' I ask.

'Aha, now I had to time travel forward a century to make that work. I thought you might have figured that out by now. You disappoint me.'

I go to messages on my phone and there's another text.

'Hi Pippa and Poppy, two peas in a pod. Look at the number when you move the spaces: 31 10 1600 613.'

It's our medieval birthday.

'Now look at it again.'

We look and it has changed to 07731 102 000.

'I wasn't absolutely sure we'd all make it back so I left that message for you.'

'Cool. Our new birth date. Will that work now?'

'Yep, that's my new mobile number so you can contact me any time. Pippa, look in the side pocket of your backpack. Now, both of you, give me a smelly hug, I have to catch a plane from Inverness before Celia misses me; there's a taxi waiting for me at the castle at 1 o'clock.'

120

'Oh thanks Uncle Tom,' Pippa yells after him as she pulls out a brand new smartphone just like mine. 'But will I still have to go up the brae?'

'No,' he shouts. 'There's a new phone mast going up near Ballindourie by the end of the month. I'm not the CEO of a communications company for nothing.'

We're back at Heather Cottage and Pippa and I agree that we've just enjoyed the best shower of our whole life (lives?). Here we are, smelling sweet, watching boring Flog it on BBC One, because there's no Sky TV, waiting for the gang to come home and wondering what on earth we're going to say about nicking prescriptions and lying to the chemist.

There's a knock at the door and in comes Caitlin.

'Are you okay, you two? A'body's talking about how you saved a mother and baby by running back for antibiotics from doon the water. What happened?'

'What are they saying, Mam?' We'll have to be very careful what we say.

'Well some woman had to be treated for septicemia and sent off by helicopter tae Raigmore Hospital.'

'Aye that's right,' Pippa says with a sidelong glance at me. 'Um...how did ye find out?'

'Sandy the chemist said thon doctor wi' the red hair dropped in at the shop wi the patient's details about 12 o'clock this morning.'

'Did the chemist ken this woman?'

'No. She was some Isabella Douglas but not from around here, and I spoke to that doctor just now, before he got in a taxi. He said ye were brilliant. Well fancy that.'

'That's us. Pippa and Poppy two peas in a pod! Finally.'

'Come on Pippa, yer dad's getting a fire going. Come and give me a hand to get some food ready. Poppy, when the two families get back, tell everyone they're invited to a barbecue say about 7 o'clock.'

'Ooh thanks, that sounds great,' I say.

But I'm feeling lost without Pippa. We've been through so much for what seems like a very long time, but in fact,was no time at all. I take the chance to message Katie with the news that I've met my actual twin and everything's good.

The evening has gone well with everyone chatting excitedly about the day's events. The boys loved their adventure park especially the canoeing and Pippa and I fib outrageously, embellishing the tale of helping a strange doctor to save the life of a gypsy woman and her baby.

The sun goes down and we look up at the clear, darkening, star-studded sky.

'Look,' Ralph shouts. 'What's that?'

'It's a shooting star,' Rosie Mum says, smiling at Pippa and me.

'She's gone to Heaven,' Pippa and I say in perfect unison. Nobody asks who.

But there's still a lot left unexplained.

Chapter 19:
Back to Normal?

Hey Guys, I'm back in London and still in one piece. But it's so hard to meet a twin you never knew and then leave her behind. I miss Pippa so-o-o much, I really do because I really like her and not seeing her makes me want to cry. Isn't that soppy?

Katie reckons it's super awesome that I have an actual twin, who isn't just virtual and untouchable, and she can't wait to meet her.

Of course, Katie doesn't know about absolutely everything; nobody except us crossovers, Pippa and me and Uncle Tom know the whole story. Whatever is behind the cave behind the bumble bee willow tree stays behind the cave behind the bumble bee willow tree. Do you remember I told you that everybody has to have a tiny secret bit that's hidden away from the world? Can you imagine which funny farm they'd stick us in if we told them what went on?

Dad, Mum and Ralph, and Caitlin and Rory just think we were very grown up to get those antibiotics to the doctor to save that woman and her baby. Thank goodness for time suspension. Wouldn't it be cool if we could use it all the time?

We got away with nicking the prescriptions, probably because the doctor's signature is so bad it could be anybody's and the chemist piles up so many prescriptions he hasn't got time to check them. What puzzles me though is where the fuzzy fairy (sorry that's a Pippaism) did that Isabella Douglas come from? I'm wondering if there's a whole other story of reincarnation bubbling away there that we'll never find out about. You never know. That gypsy, Isabella Douglas might have wanted her baby to live again just like Estelle wanted her twins to have another chance. It's totally weird to think Penelope would be dead now in 1613 if we hadn't saved the mother and baby. The other night I dreamt I'd drowned in the Loch and woke up in a sweat. Maybe, if Lady Isabel and the baby had died again, I, as Penelope, would be drowned again.

But I'm here, so we carry on in the real world, Pippa and I. Pippa loves her new smartphone and we text all the time and Skype quite often. Uncle Tom clicks off the odd text to check that we're okay but we had a three way Skype the other night with his good news. Celia's pregnant. There's going to be a new baby in the family which is quite amazing because they must be very old, like over thirty five at least if not nearly forty. Anyway it's a happy story.

I'm still missing Pippa but we can't help thinking how lucky we are. People who lose their mum in childbirth never get to meet her but we did. (We've been extra careful to delete texts on that particular subject.) And we both have caring families who seem to love us; that counts for a lot these days of family squabbles, the big D splitting up families and the big C taking parents away too soon to the rest home in the sky.

Don't listen to me; I'm thinking too much.

Pippa has terrific adoptive parents and there's no way she wants to leave them and I couldn't have a better dad and step mum; even Ralph is great, most of the time. We twins miss each other, true, but we keep in touch.

Estelle seems to be cool with this Rest in Peace stuff; there have been no voices, no pix and no texts since that escape from the cave. Zero. Even Uncle Tom hasn't heard a pip pop squeak he says. Do you think I should believe him?

I remember him saying that Estelle has vapourised so she can't have a double existence now. But didn't he say he, Philippa and I are crossovers with a double existence? I can't say I'll be sorry if we don't get another chance to cross over. It

124

was fun but I prefer sheets, pillows and duvets to scratchy wool and dusty straw and that jelly made from boiled pigs' trotters was gross.

Oh my days, I'm so excited. My school friends keep talking about 'Poppy's twin' and everybody wants to meet her so Pippa is coming to school with me at Brentgold for a whole week – but she'll have to wear uniform the Year Head says. Not a problem, I have spares and they'll fit. If you're wondering how that can happen, it's like this. Up in Scotland, half term is a week earlier than down here and it's called 'The Tattie Holidays' which is when the school pupils go and gather potatoes on the farms for a week and earn money. The tattie picking is dying out but they still have the holiday but not the wages. Ballindourie School people, it seems, are really excited about 'Pippa's twin' and she has been given the week off after half term which is *my* half term so that means two whole weeks together, and guess what comes in the middle of the second week: Halloween, our joint birthday, the day the ghost hovered and Cyber Spook wafted into my space. I wonder if she'll float back again. But who was the first ghost in Brent Cross? Was it Penelope or Philippa? And who was the ghost in Inverness? Was it Philippa or Penelope? Perhaps we'll never know.

We'll have a small family birthday party this year with *no* fancy dress thank you. Pippa agrees; she's fed up with the guising (Scotland's trick-or-treating) with Halloween masks that they have every year in Scotland, but she says she'll make a neepie (turnip) lantern just for fun. Rory and Caitlin are driving down on the Thursday, for the party on the Friday, and they'll take Pippa back to Scotland on Sunday. Ralph can have Charlie to keep him company and of course Katie must be there. She'll always be my bestie. Like Kara in Ballindourie who Pippa says is her best pal. Mind you she says, like me, she hasn't told her everything.

125

'Pippa,' I ask on Skype, 'do you think Kara can get two days off school as well? We could say she's invited to our first ever birthday party together as twins.'

'Hey that would be ace. Katie and Kara wouldn't have to feel left out and they could get to know each other. Okay Poppy, let's both check with all the parents and I'll check with my school.'

By 8 o'clock in the evening it's sorted. Everybody likes the idea so we'll have eleven at the party including Uncle Tom and Auntie Celia. Even with Bump, who's just beginning to show, we won't reach unlucky thirteen. I've got a good feeling about this party.

It's Saturday morning, October 17th 2014 and Pippa has come down on the sleeper train from Inverness and I'm meeting her at Kings Cross and we'll catch the tube home. Here she is, looking sleepy, dragging a small tartan wheeled suitcase.

'Dad's given me money to spend on clothes at Brent Cross and they're bringing a bigger case down in the car; that's my birthday present.'

'Wicked. I'll have to get my dad to do the same. Well at least that case isn't too heavy to cart through the underground.'

We chat non-stop on the train and the walk home. I ask her if she remembers being the ghost at our party and wait for a reaction. She looks puzzled.

'I think I would know if it was me, Poppy.'

'Did I say it was you?'

'No…but…'

'Uncle Tom!' we say in one voice. We'll ask him, but only when there's nobody else around.

Katie's not coming until Sunday lunch so we twins can chill all day; I show her our mum's garden and we both recognise many of the plants from the castle, 400 years ago, and tell each other we can never tell anyone about our amazing experiences.

'I wonder what they're all doing now,' I ask ourselves.

'Maybe we can ask Uncle Tom if he's still crossing over.'

'Maybe. There's so much to ask him but I'm not sure we'll get straight answers. I reckon there's a lot he hasn't told us.'

'There's something about Auntie Celia, Pippa. Do you think we might have met her in our last life?'

'I don't remember her at all.' Pippa says but I think I do.

'Come on. Mum's going to drop us off at Ally Pally. When did you last go ice-skating?'

'Huh! We've got Inverness Ice Centre, you know. I bet you can't do backward crossovers!'

'Yes I can. I bet you can't do a counter turn.'

'I can so.'

Ralph and Charlie are coming too but they're probably better skaters so we won't have to look after them. Mum's got a book to read in the Ice Café.

I hate to say it, but I think my twin is a better skater than I am but we manage a pair spin without falling over. But the boys are better than both of us so we can't get too uppity.

We're all ravenous when we finish and beg Mum for a treat. I like the hot chocolate with marshmallow at the Ice Café and Ralph fancies a pizza. So we all end up having pizzas, a drink and doughnuts. Mum's sighing but I know she's secretly pleased she doesn't have to go home and cook for us.

That evening Uncle Tom, Celia and Bump come over to let Mum and Dad go out but we can't get him alone so we leave him and Celia watching catch up TV after Ralph goes to bed and decide to work on a Facebook account for Pippa who's quite new to social media. I tell her it's because she lives in the sticks.

'The sticks aren't so bad. At least people speak to each other, instead of fiddle, fiddle, fiddle on their mobiles and iPads,' Pippa yells back at me but we're laughing. We use my smartphone for a profile picture but it looks too much like me

127

so we get Uncle Tom to take a picture of us both together. Then we fool about taking pictures of each other and Uncle Tom and Auntie Celia.

'Auntie Celia,' Pippa says. 'I've just noticed how bright blue your eyes are; they go with your blue-black hair. I like that.'

'Thank you,' she says before Uncle Tom chips in a little too quickly. 'A word of warning girls. We've got secrets. Take care with Facebook and WhatsApp and don't even go near a tweet.'

'We can enjoy them a bit though if we're sensible,' I say. Think of all these twin tricks.'

'School's gonna be fun,' Pippa adds.

'You're never going to be able to fool your teachers,' Uncle Tom says. 'You're not identical.' He means my birthmark but I have a plan so I ring Katie and ask her to bring one of her mum's pan sticks. She's got so many she won't miss one. I think it might work; our dad says you could scrape off her makeup with a spoon.

We try it the next day and it hides the butterfly completely but you can see the patch of stuff.

'I know what to do,' says Pippa and she clarts it over her own face at the same place. Katie giggles with delight.

'I can only tell the difference because of your clothes now, until you speak of course. Poppy, maybe you could try to speak Scots and Pippa you could try the London accent.'

'Oh, I'm no good at posh,' says Pippa.

'Well practise,' says Katie.

'And I'm useless at an Inverness accent,' I say. All the same, after Katie goes home, we spend ages recording our voices until we're not at all bad at swapping our accents. Roll on Monday morning registration.

We're walking to school chatting about Scotland.

'Do you remember when Robbie at the castle thought I was you?'

'Aye, I mind fine – oops I have to be posh – yes I remember it well. We'll never be able to do that again.'

'Didn't he see the birthmark?'

'Maybe he thought it was jam on my face, which wouldn't be unusual. Hey, d'ye think everybody knows I'm coming?'

'No way; only my Form Tutor Mr Patel knows and some of the teachers, and I don't know who Katie has told.'

'This could raise a few laughs. Listen ...'

We manage to catch out a few people in the crowd along the road outside the school and walking across the school grounds. Pippa goes first, looking a bit dreamy and distracted and when somebody I know says hi she says a dozy hi and walks on. I'm following on about ten feet behind and I jump on them all bubbly with all the questions:

'Hi Anu, how was the weekend?'

'But, but ... huh?'

'What's up Mo?'

'Eh... didn't I just see you?'

The faces are a picture. I wish Pippa could see them but we'll swap when we get to the girls' loo, which I see she's just dived into. I join her and we change over. I go first and when I meet someone I know I say hi and pretend I'm in a hurry and walk on. When Pippa sees who I've been talking to she stops them.

'Hi. I'm new. What's your name?'

'You joking me Poppy?'

'Hi. Can you tell me where the girls' loo is, please? I'm new today.'

'Are you sure you're ok, Poppy?' We're loving the puzzled faces.

Then I catch her up and we walk to registration arm in arm. My form love this whole joke and they egg us on to play a twin trick on Mr Patel.

'Hey, Poppy's twin whatever your name is...'

'Pippa.'

'Right Pippa; you go and hide behind the cupboard, right, and Poppy, you sit here, right and we'll leave an empty seat beside you next to the cupboard, right, and when he's not looking Pippa, you slip out and sit next to Poppy, right, then...'

'Okay, Jordan, we get it... right,' I say and Mr Patel walks in hitting his iPad for the register.

'Take your seats please, for the register,' he says with a twinkle. I think we've been rumbled but he starts reading the names out in surname alphabetical order.

'Gareth... Poppy, Jack, Gemma, Dwayne, Miresh...' he goes on and turns his back on the class... 'Suzy, Billy, Ryo...' and by this time Pippa has sat down next to me and he doesn't seem to have seen her.

'Maria, Chi ... and Xanthe.' By this time the class can't keep their giggles in.' 'And Pippa, of course; you'll have to get up very early to catch me but a nice try.'

Ah well, it was fun while it lasted. The week flies by and we play a few tricks but we're both rubbish at changing our accents so they mostly don't work. Pippa comes to all my lessons and she's pretty smart so we don't get picked on.

A cheeky 'You a Jock then?' gets an even cheekier 'No, I'm a Pippa' and that stops *him* in his tracks. Then we overhear, 'Them twin chicks are buff but I bet they'd get proper lairy if they switched on you.'

'You better believe it,' my sister says. 'Ye dinna want to see me in a hissy fit.'

'What did she say?'

'She said you don't want to see her proper vexed,' I say, 'so leg it.' He does which is a surprise but not before he sends back, 'YOLO!'

'But we've lived twice,' we whisper.

'YOLT!' we yell back and yes, you've got it, in unison.

Nearly everybody's fascinated by our story that we hadn't seen each other since we were a few weeks old.

'What about your rents? How could that happen?'

'Our mum died when we were born and we got split up because our dad couldn't look after both of us.'

'That's dred. Sorry about that.'

'But it's all good now we've found each other,' I say. 'We'll always have somebody to roll with.'

'Safe.'

'Excellent.'

'Yeah but it's random, in-it?'

'Nim, nim, nim.'

Pippa's keeping quiet but when we get on the road home she bursts out, '*What* was that last bit about?'

'We're good, we're weird and no, that's rubbish, we're not.'

'Are we?'

'What?'

'Weird?'

'Probably.'

Happy days. Half term comes and we shop and don't drop, go bowling, skating again and to the cinema, before Caitlin, Rory and Kara arrive and it's time for our Halloween birthday party.

Katie likes Kara which is great and we all plan silly games that don't involve ghosts; it all goes swimmingly and we sleep peacefully.

Celia's excited about her baby, due in late April 2015, but Uncle Tom's being a bit quiet. We make plans for Pippa and her mum and dad to come to London next summer to see the

131

baby and Dad, Mum, Ralph and I are having Christmas in London and going up to spend Hogmanay with Pippa, Caitlin and Rory at the castle. They reckon Dad will be a lucky first footer with his dark hair.

Uncle Tom and Auntie Celia are invited but Uncle Tom says they can't make it to Ballindourie. I suspect Auntie Celia is disappointed.

Time slips by; Hogmanay is brilliant in the big ballroom in the castle. The men wear kilts and most of the women wear long dresses. Pippa and I are identical in cream silk dresses and green pumps. Somebody says we look medieval which makes us both catch our breath for a second. All is calm and happy. Not a whistle from the parallel existence.

...

Fast forward to May the 1st: the babies were born at two o'clock this morning and one of them is struggling. Uncle Tom says he'll ring later. Yes, I *did* say babies; Celia had twins. I suppose they run in the family.

My mind is going back to Estelle taking me on our midwives' round to visit pregnant Aunt Sarah and her two little ones and blue-eyed, black haired Aunt Cecily and her four month old May Day baby boy. I know why Pippa thought she had never met Celia. She hadn't met Cecily but *I* had. I don't have to be told what is about to happen.

'We lost one twin,' Uncle Tom tells us on the speaker phone, 'but the little boy is doing well. We've called him Alastair.'

'How is Celia?' Dad asks.

'She's absolutely fine, thank goodness.'

'And did you name the other little boy?' I ask, deviously. The others are stunned by the answer I was expecting.

'It was a girl. We called her Penelope because she had your butterfly birthmark on her cheek.'

132

Chapter 20:
2026 - Limboland?

I'm off to pick up my two year old twins from nursery soon. Yes, more twins. They are boys this time, Iain and Gordon, dark haired and brown-eyed like their father with no complications, so far, like butterfly birthmarks or imaginary, ghostlike companions. By the way, I'm a midwife, when I get time off from being a busy mum, and I practise reflexology in my spare time.

Pippa lives nearby with her husband and children, three year old Rory and one year old Caitlin, named after their grandparents who have moved into a retirement village five miles away since they left service. Ballindourie Castle is now a 5* hotel, by the way, if you fancy an expensive holiday. She's a fashion designer and she bakes wonderful wedding cakes to order.

Ralph is twenty now and studying geomorphology of all things and Mum and Dad are still at the old house. Rosie Mum loves to grow all kinds of vegetables in the herb garden but she's given up the health shop. Dad has taken up fishing and golf but still works part time. Uncle Tom and Auntie Celia have lots of holidays in Scotland and twelve year old Alastair now has a sister called Abby, who's ten. Uncle Tom is a director of several mobile communications groups now, which doesn't surprise me.

Life is good but memories of all those strange happenings linger on. Did it all really happen?

Thirteen years later, I've still kept my old smartphone and there's one conversation thread I'd like you to read. The messages came through to me in my bedroom that night we heard that Celia's baby girl had died. They came to me alone and not Pippa. I haven't shared it with her. Do you think I should?

'Alastair misses Penelope.'
'Is that you Estelle?' I text.
'Have you forgotten? She left Limboland. It's Tam.'
'Is baby Penelope in Limboland?'
'She's back in 1615. She'll be a playmate for the new wee baron at the castle.'
'So you wanted one child here and one child there!!'
'If you like.'
'Did you die a natural death, Uncle Tom? I never asked you that.'
'No. There was an accident. A tree fell on me.'
'Am I in Limboland?'
'No Poppy, not at the moment, but...'
'But what?'
'Bye.'
'And what about Pippa?'

Since then I've never been able to get an answer out of my infuriating uncle but perhaps that's for the best. I try ringing his new number from time to time, 01052 015 095 but all I get is: *'You've dialled an incorrect number. Please check the number and try again.'* Perhaps at least one of Celia's twins will live to 80, I'm guessing.

There's one thing I did share with Pippa, however, and I'd like to share it with you now. When I was clearing out my room before going off to Uni, I found two things in my old backpack: a box for some antibiotics prescribed in August 2013 and inside the box, not the capsules, but a gold pendant set with garnets and pearls. I told Baron Gavin I'd treasure it forever, and I will.

***

Author's Note

Eliza Jane Goés has published three books of fictionalised memoir reflecting on how migration has influenced cultural integration over the past 60 years: *Fusion, The Cosmopolites and The Not Quite English Teacher.* She has also written many short stories and poems, several of which have been published.

She has retired from a long teaching career in Fochabers in Scotland, Kenya, Zambia and London, including Hendon School. She now lives in Hampshire with her husband, not too far from the grandchildren. The children in the Robins class at The Holme C of E Primary School, Headley, where she helps with their reading, have named her Mrs Gogo, which is fine. She continues to write stories and poems.

www.elizajanegoesahead.com

136

Printed in Great Britain
by Amazon

57091632R00081